SCANNERS
AND OTHERS
THREE SCIENCE FICTION STORIES

SCANNERS
AND OTHERS
THREE SCIENCE FICTION STORIES

CORDWAINER SMITH

WILDSIDE PRESS

SCANNERS AND OTHERS:
THREE SCIENCE FICTION STORIES

"Scanners Live in Vain" originally appeared in *Fantasy Book* in 1950. "The Game of Rat and Dragon" originally appeared in *Galaxy*, October 1955. "Mark Elf" originally appeared in *Saturn Science Fiction*, May 1957.

Published in 2010 by Wildside Press.

CONTENTS

SCANNERS LIVE IN VAIN

MARTEL WAS ANGRY. He did not even adjust his blood away from anger. He stamped across the room by judgment, not by sight. When he saw the table hit the floor, and could tell by the expression on Luci's face that the table must have made a loud crash, he looked down to see if his leg was broken. It was not. Scanner to the core, he had to scan himself. The action was reflex and automatic. The inventory included his legs, abdomen, chest-box of instruments, hands, arms, face, and back with the mirror. Only then did Martel go back to being angry. He talked with his voice, even though he knew that his wife hated its blare and preferred to have him write.

"I tell you, I must cranch. I have to cranch. It's my worry, isn't it?" When Luci answered, he saw only a part of her words as he read her lips: "Darling . . . you're my husband . . . right to love you . . . dangerous . . . do it . . . dangerous . . . wait . . ."

He faced her, but put sound in his voice, letting the blare hurt her again: "I tell you, I'm going to cranch."

Catching her expression, he became rueful and a little tender: "Can't you understand what it means to me? To get out of this horrible prison in my own head? To be a man again — hearing your voice, smelling smoke? To *feel* again — to feel my feet on the ground, to feel the air move against my face? Don't you know what it means?"

Her wide-eyed worrisome concern thrust him back into pure annoyance. He read only a few words as her lips moved: ". . . love you for your own good . . . don't you think I want you to be human? . . . your own good . . . too much . . . he said . . . they said . . ."

When he roared at her, he realized that his voice must be particularly bad. He knew that the sound hurt her no less than did the words: "Do you think I wanted you to marry a scanner? Didn't I tell you we're almost as low as the habermans? We're dead, I tell you. We've got to be dead to do our work. How can anybody go to the up-and-out? Can you dream what raw space is? I warned you.

But you married me. All right, you married a man. Please, darling, let me be a man. Let me hear your voice, let me feel the warmth of being alive, of being human. Let me!"

He saw by her look of stricken assent that he had won the argument. He did not use his voice again. Instead, he pulled his tablet up from where it hung against his chest. He wrote on it, using the pointed fingernail of his right forefinger — the talking nail of a scanner — in quick, cleancut script: *Pls, drlng, whrs crnching wire?*

She pulled the long gold-sheathed wire out of the pocket of her apron. She let its field sphere fall to the carpeted floor. Swiftly, dutifully, with the deft obedience of a scanner's wife, she wound the cranching wire around his head, spirally around his neck and chest. She avoided the instruments set in his chest. She even avoided the radiating scars around the instruments, the stigmata of men who had gone up and into the out. Mechanically he lifted a foot as she slipped the wire between his feet. She drew the wire taut. She snapped the small plug into the high-burden control next to his heart-reader. She helped him to sit down, arranging his hands for him, pushing his head back into the cup at the top of the chair. She turned then, full-face toward him, so that he could read her lips easily. Her expression was composed.

She knelt, scooped up the sphere at the other end of the wire, stood erect calmly, her back to him. He scanned her, and saw nothing in her posture but grief which would have escaped the eye of anyone but a scanner. She spoke: he could see her chest-muscles moving. She realized that she was not facing him, and turned so that he could see her lips.

"Ready at last?"

He smiled a *yes.*

She turned her back to him again. (Luci could never bear to watch him go under the wire.) She tossed the wire-sphere into the air. It caught in the force-field, and hung there. Suddenly it glowed. That was all. All — except for the sudden red stinking roar of coming back to his senses. Coming back, across the wild threshold of pain.

When he awakened, under the wire, he did not feel as though

he had just cranched. Even though it was the second cranching within the week, he felt fit. He lay in the chair. His ears drank in the sound of air touching things in the room. He heard Luci breathing in the next room, where she was hanging up the wire to cool. He smelt the thousand and one smells that are in anybody's room: the crisp freshness of the germ-burner, the sour-sweet tang of the humidifier, the odor of the dinner they had just eaten, the smells of clothes, furniture, of people themselves. All these were pure delight. He sang a phrase or two of his favorite song:

> *"Here's to the haberman, up-and-out!*
> *"Up — oh! — and out — oh! — up-and-out! . . .*

He heard Luci chuckle in the next room. He gloated over the sounds of her dress as she swished to the doorway.

She gave him her crooked little smile. "You sound all right. Are you all right, really?"

Even with this luxury of senses, he scanned. He took the flash-quick inventory which constituted his professional skill. His eyes swept in the news of the instruments. Nothing showed off scale, beyond the nerve compression hanging in the edge of Danger. But he could not worry about the nerve-box. That always came through cranching. You couldn't get under the wire without having it show on the nerve-box. Some day the box would go to *Overload* and drop back down to *Dead.* That was the way a haberman ended. But you couldn't have everything. People who went to the up-and-out had to pay the price for space.

Anyhow, he should worry! He was a scanner. A good one, and he knew it. If he couldn't scan himself, who could? This cranching wasn't too dangerous. Dangerous, but not too dangerous.

Luci put out her hand and ruffled his hair as if she had been reading his thoughts, instead of just following them: "But you know you shouldn't have! You shouldn't!"

"But I did!" He grinned at her.

Her gaiety still forced, she said: "Come on, darling, let's have a good time. I have almost everything there is in the icebox — all your favorite tastes. And I have two new records just full of smells. I tried them out myself, and even I liked them. And you know me —"

"Which?"

"Which what, you old darling?"

He slipped his hand over her shoulders as he limped out of the room. (He could never go back to feeling the floor beneath his feet, feeling the air against his face, without being bewildered and clumsy. As if cranching was real, and being a haberman was a bad dream. But he *was* a haberman, and a scanner. "You know what I meant, Luci.

the smells, which you have. Which one did you like, on the record?"

"Well-l-l," said she, judiciously, "there were some lamb chops that were the strangest things —"

He interrupted: "What are lambtchots?"

"Wait till you smell them. Then guess. I'll tell you this much. It's a smell hundreds and hundreds of years old. They found out about it in the old books."

"Is a lambtchot a beast?"

"I won't tell you. You've got to wait," she laughed, as she helped him sit down and spread his tasting dishes before him. He wanted to go back over the dinner first, sampling all the pretty things he had eaten, and savoring them this time with his now-living lips and tongue.

When Luci had found the music wire and had thrown its sphere up into the force-field, he reminded her of the new smells. She took out the long glass records and set the first one into a transmitter.

"Now sniff!"

A queer, frightening, exciting smell came over the room. It seemed like nothing in this world, nor like anything from the up-and-out. Yet it was familiar. His mouth watered. His pulse beat a little faster; he scanned his heartbox. (Faster, sure enough.) But that smell, what was it? In mock perplexity, he grabbed her hands, looked into her eyes, and growled:

"Tell me, darling! Tell me, or I'll eat you up!"

"That's just right!"

"What?"

"You're right. It should make you want to eat me. It's meat."

"Meat. Who?"

"Not a person," said she, knowledgeably, "a Beast. A Beast which people used to eat. A lamb was a small sheep — you've seen sheep out in the Wild, haven't you? — and a chop is part of its middle — here!" She pointed at her chest.

Martel did not hear her. All his boxes had swung over toward *Alarm,* some to *Danger.* He fought against the roar of his own mind, forcing his body into excess excitement. How easy it was to be a scanner when you really stood outside your own body, haberman-fashion, and looked back into it with your eyes alone. Then you could manage the body, rule it coldly even in the enduring agony of space. But to realize that you *were* a body, that this thing was ruling you, that the mind could kick the flesh and send it roaring off into panic! That was bad.

He tried to remember the days before he had gone into the haberman device, before he had been cut apart for the up-and-out. Had he always been subject to the rush of his emotions from his mind to his body, from his body back to his mind, confounding him so that he couldn't scan? But he hadn't been a scanner then.

He knew what had hit him. Amid the roar of his own pulse, he knew. In the nightmare of the up-and-out, that smell had forced its way through to him, while their ship burned off Venus and the habermans fought the collapsing metal with their bare hands. He had scanned then: all were in *Danger.* Chestboxes went up to *Overload* and dropped to *Dead* all around him as he had moved from man to man, shoving the drifting corpses out of his way as he fought to scan each man in turn, to clamp vises on unnoticed broken legs, to snap the sleeping valve on men whose instruments showed they were hopelessly near *Overload.* With men trying to work and cursing him for a scanner while he, professional zeal aroused, fought to do his job and keep them alive in the great pain of space, he had smelled that smell. It had fought its way along his rebuilt nerves, past the haberman cuts, past all the safeguards of physical and mental discipline. In the wildest hour of tragedy, he had smelled aloud. He remembered it was like a bad cranching, connected with the fury and nightmare all around him. He had even stopped his work to scan himself, fearful that the first effect might come, breaking past all haberman cuts and ruining him with the pain of space. But he had come through. His own instruments stayed and stayed at *Danger,* without nearing *Overload.* He had done his job, and won a commendation for it. He had even forgotten the burning ship.

All except the smell.

And here the smell was all over again — the smell of meat-withfire.

Luci looked at him with wifely concern. She obviously thought he had cranched too much, and was about to haberman back. She tried to be cheerful: "You'd better rest, honey."

He whispered to her: "Cut — off — that — smell."

She did not question his word. She cut the transmitter. She even crossed the room and stepped up the room controls until a small breeze flitted across the floor and drove the smells up to the ceiling.

He rose, tired and stiff. (His instruments were normal, except that heart was fast and nerves still hanging on the edge of *Danger.*) He spoke sadly:

"Forgive me, Luci. I suppose I shouldn't have cranched. Not so soon again. But darling, I have to get out from being a haberman. How can I ever be near you? How can I be a man — not hearing my own voice, not even feeling my own life as it goes through my veins? I love you, darling. Can't I ever be near you?"

Her pride was disciplined and automatic: "But you're a scanner!"

"I know I'm a scanner. But so what?"

She went over the words, like a tale told a thousand times to reassure herself: "You are the bravest of the brave, the most skillful of the skilled. All mankind owes most honor to the scanner, who unites the Earths of mankind. Scanners are the protectors of the habermans. They are the judges in the up-and-out. They make men live in the place where men need desperately to die. They are the most honored of mankind, and even the chiefs of the Instrumentality are delighted to pay them homage!"

With obstinate sorrow he demurred: "Luci, we've heard that all before. But does it pay us back —"

"Scanners work for more than pay. They are the strong guards of mankind.' Don't you remember that?"

"But our lives, Luci. What can you get out of being the wife of a scanner? Why did you marry me? I'm human only when I cranch. The rest of the time — you know what I am. A machine. A man turned into a machine. A man who has been killed and kept alive for duty. Don't you realize what I miss?"

"Of course, darling, of course —"

He went on: "Don't you think I remember my childhood? Don't you think I remember what it is to be a man and not a haberman? To walk and feel my feet on the ground? To feel a decent clean pain instead of watching my body every minute to see if I'm alive? How will I know if I'm dead? Did you ever think of that, Luci? How will I know if I'm dead?"

She ignored the unreasonableness of his outburst. Pacifyingly, she said: "Sit down, darling. Let me make you some kind of a drink. You're overwrought."

Automatically, he scanned. "No I'm not! Listen to me. How do you think it feels to be in the up-and-out with the crew tied-for-space all around you? How do you think it feels to watch them sleep? How do you think I like scanning, scanning, scanning month after month, when I can feel the pain of space beating against every part of my body, trying to get past my haberman blocks? How do you think I like to wake the men when I have to, and have them hate me for it? Have you ever seen habermans fight — strong men fighting, and neither knowing pain, fighting until one touches *Overload?* Do you think about that, Luci?" Triumphantly he added: "Can you blame me if I cranch, and come back to being a man, just two days a month?"

"I'm not blaming you, darling. Let's enjoy your cranch. Sit down now, and have a drink."

He was sitting down, resting his face in his hands, while she fixed the drink, using natural fruits out of bottles in addition to the secure alkaloids. He watched her restlessly and pitied her for marrying a scanner; and then, though it was unjust, resented having to pity her.

Just as she turned to hand him the drink, they both jumped a little as the phone rang. It should not have rung. They had turned it off. It rang again, obviously on the emergency circuit. Stepping ahead of Luci, Martel strode over to the phone and looked into it. Vomact was looking at him.

The custom of scanners entitled him to be brusque, even with a senior scanner, on certain given occasions. This was one.

Before Vomact could speak, Martel spoke two words into the plate, not caring whether the old man could read lips or not:

"Cranching. Busy."

He cut the switch and went back to Luci.

The phone rang again.

Luci said, gently, "I can find out what it is, darling. Here, take your drink and sit down."

"Leave it alone," said her husband. "No one has a right to call when I'm cranching. He knows that. He ought to know that."

The phone rang again. In a fury, Martel rose and went to the plate. He cut it back on. Vomact was on the screen. Before Martel could speak, Vomact held up his talking nail in line with his heart-box. Martel reverted to discipline:

"Scanner Martel present and waiting, sir."

The lips moved solemnly: "Top emergency."

"Sir, I am under the wire."

"Top emergency."

"Sir, don't you understand?" Martel mouthed his words, so he could be sure that Vomact followed. "I . . . am . . . under . . . the . . . wire. Unfit . . . for . . . Space!"

Vomact repeated: "Top emergency. Report to Central Tie-in."

"But, sir, no emergency like this —"

"Right, Martel. No emergency like this, ever before. Report to Tiein." With a faint glint of kindliness, Vomact added: "No need to decranch. Report as you are."

This time it was Martel whose phone was cut out. The screen went gray.

He turned to Luci. The temper had gone out of his voice. She came to him. She kissed him, and rumpled his hair. All she could say was,

"I'm sorry."

She kissed him again, knowing his disappointment. "Take good care of yourself, darling. I'll wait."

He scanned, and slipped into his transparent aircoat. At the window he paused, and waved. She called, "Good luck!" As the air flowed past him he said to himself,

"This is the first time I've felt flight in — eleven years. Lord, but it's easy to fly if you can feel yourself live!"

Central Tie-in glowed white and austere far ahead. Martel peered. He saw no glare of incoming ships from the up-and-out, no shuddering flare of space-fire out of control. Everything was quiet, as it should be on an off-duty night.

And yet Vomact had called. He had called an emergency higher than Space. There was no such thing. But Vomact had called it.

When Martel got there, he found about half the scanners present, two dozen or so of them. He lifted the talking finger. Most of the scanners were standing face to face, talking in pairs as they read lips. A few of the old, impatient ones were scribbling on their tablets and then thrusting the tablets into other people's faces. All the faces wore the dull dead relaxed look of a haberman. When Martel entered the room, he knew that most of the others laughed in the deep isolated privacy of their own minds, each thinking things it would be useless to express in formal words. It had been a long time since a scanner showed up at a meeting cranched.

Vomact was not there: probably, thought Martel, he was still on the phone calling others. The light of the phone flashed on and off; the bell rang. Martel felt odd when he realized that of all those present, he was the only one to hear that loud bell. It made him realize why ordinary people did not like to be around groups of habermans or scanners. Martel looked around for company.

His friend Chang was there, busy explaining to some old and testy scanner that he did not know why Vomact had called. Martel looked farther and saw Parizianski. He walked over, threading his way past the others with a dexterity that showed he could feel his feet from the inside, and did not have to watch them. Several of the others stared at him with their dead faces, and tried to smile.

But they lacked full muscular control and their faces twisted into horrid masks. (Scanners usually knew better than to show expression on faces which they could no longer govern. Martel added to himself, *I swear* I'll *never smile again unless I'm cranched.*)

Parizianski gave him the sign of the talking finger. Looking face to face, he spoke:

"You come here cranched?"

Parizianski could not hear his own voice, so the words roared like the words on a broken and screeching phone; Martel was startled, but knew that the inquiry was well meant. No one could be better-natured than the burly Pole.

"Vomact called. Top emergency."

"You told him you were cranched?"

"Yes."

"He still made you come?"

"Then all this — it is not for Space? You could not go up-and-out? You are like ordinary men?"

"That's right."

"Then why did he call us?" Some pre-haberman habit made Parizianski wave his arms in inquiry. The hand struck the back of the old man behind them. The slap could be heard throughout the room, but only Martel heard it. Instinctively, he scanned Parizianski and the old scanner, and they scanned him back. Only then did the old man ask why Martel had scanned him. When Martel explained that he was under the wire, the old man moved swiftly away to pass on the news that there was a cranched scanner present at the tie-in.

Even this minor sensation could not keep the attention of most of the scanners from the worry about the top emergency. One young man, who had scanned his first transit just the year before, dramatically interposed himself between Parizianski and Martel. He dramatically flashed his tablet at them:

Is Vmct mad?

The older men shook their heads. Martel, remembering that it had not been too long that the young man had been haberman, mitigated the dead solemnity of the denial with a friendly smile. He spoke in a normal voice, saying:

"Vomact is the senior of scanners. I am sure that he could not go mad. Would he not see it on his boxes first?"

Martel had to repeat the question, speaking slowly and mouthing his words before the young scanner could understand the comment. The young man tried to make his face smile, and twisted it into a comic mask. But he took up his tablet and scribbled:

Yr rght.

Chang broke away from his friend and came over, his half-Chinese face gleaming in the warm evening. (It's strange, thought Martel, that more Chinese don't become scanners. Or not so strange perhaps, if you think that they never fill their quota of habermans. Chinese love good living too much. The ones who do scan are all good ones.) Chang saw that Martel was cranched, and spoke with voice:

"You break precedents. Luci must be angry to lose you?"

"She took it well. Chang, that's strange."

"I'm cranched, and I can hear. Your voice sounds all right. How did you learn to talk like — like an ordinary person?"

"I practiced with soundtracks. Funny you noticed it. I think I am the only scanner in or between the Earths who can pass for an ordinary man. Mirrors and soundtracks. I found out how to act."

"But you don't . . ."

"No. I don't feel, or taste, or hear, or smell things, any more than you do. Talking doesn't do me much good. But I notice that it cheers up the people around me."

"It would make a difference in the life of Luci."

Chang nodded sagely. "My father insisted on it. He said, `You may be proud of being a scanner. I am sorry you are not a man. Conceal your defects.' So I tried. I wanted to tell the old boy about the up-and-out, and what we did there, but it did not matter. He said, `Airplanes were good enough for Confucius, and they are for me too.' The old humbug! He tries so hard to be a Chinese when he can't even read Old Chinese. But he's got wonderful good sense, and for somebody going on two hundred he certainly gets around."

Martel smiled at the thought: "In his airplane?"

Chang smiled back. This discipline of his facial muscles was amazing; a bystander would not think that Chang was a haber-man, controlling his eyes, cheeks, and lips by cold intellectual control. The expression had the spontaneity of life. Martel felt a flash of envy for Chang when he looked at the dead cold faces of Parizianski and the others. He knew that he himself looked fine: but why shouldn't he? He was cranched. Turning to Parizianski he said,

"Did you see what Chang said about his father? The old boy uses an airplane."

Parizianski made motions with his mouth, but the sounds meant nothing. He took up his tablet and showed it to Martel and Chang.

Bzz bzz, Ha ha. Gd *ol' boy.*

At that moment, Martel heard steps out in the corridor. He could not help looking toward the door. Other eyes followed the direction of his glance.

Vomact came in.

The group shuffled to attention in four parallel lines. They scanned one another. Numerous hands reached across to adjust the electrochemical controls on chestboxes which had begun to load up. One scanner held out a broken finger which his counter-scanner had discovered, and submitted it for treatment and splint-ing.

Vomact had taken out his staff of office. The cube at the top flashed red light through the room, the lines reformed, and all scanners gave the sign meaning, *Present and ready!*

Vomact countered with the stance signifying, *I am the senior and take command.*

Talking fingers rose in the counter-gesture, *We concur and commit ourselves.*

Vomact raised his right arm, dropped the wrist as though it were broken, in a queer searching gesture, meaning: *Any men around? Any habermans not tied? All clear for the scanners?*

Alone of all those present, the cranched Martel heard the queer rustle of feet as they all turned completely around without leaving position, looking sharply at one another and flashing their belt-lights into the dark corners of the great room. When again they faced Vomact, he made a further sign:

All clear. Follow my words.

Martel noticed that he alone relaxed. The others could not know the meaning of relaxation with the minds blocked off up there in their skulls, connected only with the eyes, and the rest of the body connected with the mind only by controlling non-sensory nerves and the instrument boxes on their chests. Martel realized that, cranched as he was, he had expected to hear Vomact's voice: the senior had been talking for some time. No sound escaped his lips. (Vomact never bothered with sound.)

". . . and when the first men to go up-and-out went to the moon, what did they find?"

"Nothing," responded the silent chorus of lips.

"Therefore they went farther, to Mars and to Venus. The ships went out year by year, but they did not come back until the Year One of Space. Then did a ship come back with the first effect. Scanners, I ask you, what is the first effect?"

"No one knows. No one knows."

"No one will ever know. Too many are the variables. By what do we know the first effect?"

"By the great pain of space," came the chorus.

"And by what further sign?"

"By the need, oh the need for death."

Vomact again: "And who stopped the need for death?"

"Henry Haberman conquered the first effect, in the Year Eighty-three of Space."

"And, Scanners, I ask you, what did he do?"

"He made the habermans."

"How, O Scanners, are habermans made?"

"They are made with the cuts. The brain is cut from the heart, the lungs. The brain is cut from the ears, the nose. The brain is cut from the mouth, the belly. The brain is cut from desire, and pain. The brain is cut from the world. Save for the eyes. Save for the control of the living flesh."

"And how, O Scanners, is flesh controlled?"

"By the boxes set in the flesh, the controls set in the chest, the signs made to rule the living body, the signs by which the body lives."

"How does a haberman live and live?"

"The haberman lives by control of the boxes."

"Whence come the habermans?"

Martel felt in the coming response a great roar of broken voices echoing through the room as the scanners, habermans themselves, put sound behind their mouthings:

"Habermans are the scum of mankind. Habermans are the weak, the cruel, the credulous, and the unfit. Habermans are the sentencedto-more-than-death. Habermans live in the mind alone. They are killed for space but they live for space. They master the ships that connect the Earths. They live in the great pain while ordinary men sleep in the cold, cold sleep of the transit."

"Brothers and Scanners, I ask you now: are we habermans or are we not?"

"We are habermans in the flesh. We are cut apart, brain and flesh. We are ready to go to the up-and-out. All of us have gone through the haberman device."

"We are habermans then?" Vomact's eyes flashed and glittered as he asked the ritual question.

Again the chorused answer was accompanied by a roar of voices heard only by Martel: "Habermans we are, and more, and more. We are the chosen who are habermans by our own free will. We are the agents of the Instrumentality of Mankind."

"What must the others say to us?"

"They must say to us, `You are the bravest of the brave, the most skillful of the skilled. All mankind owes most honor to the scanner, who unites the Earths of mankind. Scanners are the protectors of the habermans. They are the judges in the up-and-out. They make men live in the place where men need desperately to die. They are the most honored of mankind, and even the chiefs of the Instrumentality are delighted to pay them homage!'"

Vomact stood more erect: "What is the secret duty of the scanner?"

"To keep secret our law, and to destroy the acquirers thereof."

"How to destroy?"

"Twice to the *Overload,* back and *Dead.*"

"If habermans die, what the duty then?"

The scanners all compressed their lips for answer. (Silence was the code.) Martel, who — long familiar with the code — was a little bored with the proceedings, noticed that Chang was breathing too heavily; he reached over and adjusted Chang's lung-control and received the thanks of Chang's eyes. Vomact observed the interruption and glared at them both. Martel relaxed, trying to imitate the dead cold stillness of the others. It was so hard to do, when you were cranched.

"If others die, what the duty then?" asked Vomact.

"Scanners together inform the Instrumentality. Scanners together accept the punishment. Scanners together settle the case."

"And if the punishment be severe?"

"Then no ships go."

"And if scanners be not honored?"

"Then no ships go."

"And if a scanner goes unpaid?"

"Then no ships go."

"And if the Others and the Instrumentality are not in all ways at all times mindful of their proper obligation to the scanners?"

"Then no ships go."

"And what, 0 Scanners, if no ships go?"

"The Earths fall apart. The Wild comes back in. The Old Machines and the Beasts return."

"What is the first known duty of a scanner?"

"Not to sleep in the up-and-out."

"What is the second duty of a scanner?"

"To keep forgotten the name of fear."

"What is the third duty of a scanner?"

"To use the wire of Eustace Cranch only with care, only with moderation." Several pair of eyes looked quickly at Martel before the mouthed chorus went on. "To cranch only at home, only among friends, only for the purpose of remembering, of relaxing, or of begetting."

"What is the word of the scanner?"

"Faithful though surrounded by death."

"What is the motto of the scanner?"

"Awake though surrounded by silence."

"What is the work of the scanner?"

"Labor even in the heights of the up-and-out, loyalty even in the depths of the Earths."

"How do you know a scanner?"

"We know ourselves. We are dead though we live. And we talk with the tablet and the nail."

"What is this code?"

"This code is the friendly ancient wisdom of scanners, briefly put that we may be mindful and be cheered by our loyalty to one another."

At this point the formula should have run: "We complete the code. Is there work or word for the scanners?" But Vomact said, and he repeated:

"Top emergency. Top emergency."

They gave him the sign, *Present and ready!*

He said, with every eye straining to follow his lips:

"Some of you know the work of Adam Stone?"

Martel saw lips move, saying: "The Red Asteroid. The Other who lives at the edge of Space."

"Adam Stone has gone to the Instrumentality, claiming success for his work He says that he has found how to screen out the pain of space. He says that the up-and-out can be made safe for ordinary men to work in, to stay awake in. He says that there need be no more scanners."

Beltlights flashed on all over the room as scanners sought the right to speak. Vomact nodded to one of the older men. "Scanner Smith will speak."

Smith stepped slowly up into the light, watching his own feet. He turned so that they could see his face. He spoke: "I say that this is a lie. I say that Stone is a liar. I say that the Instrumentality must not be deceived."

He paused. Then, in answer to some question from the audience which most of the others did not see, he said:

"I invoke the secret duty of the scanners."

Smith raised his right hand for emergency attention:

"I say that Stone must die."

Martel, still cranched, shuddered as he heard the boos, groans, shouts, squeaks, grunts and moans which came from the scanners who forgot noise in their excitement and strove to make their dead bodies talk to one another's deaf ears. Beltlights flashed wildly all over the room. There was a rush for the rostrum and scanners milled around at the top, vying for attention until Parizianski — by sheer bulk — shoved the others aside and down, and turned to mouth at the group.

"Brother Scanners, I want your eyes."

The people on the floor kept moving, with their numb bodies jostling one another. Finally Vomact stepped up in front of Parizianski, faced the others, and said:

"Scanners, be scanners! Give him your eyes."

Parizianski was not good at public speaking. His lips moved too fast. He waved his hands, which took the eyes of the others away from his lips. Nevertheless, Martel was able to follow most of the message:

"I can't do this. Stone may have succeeded. If he has succeeded, it means the end of the scanners. It means the end of the habermans, too. None of us will have to fight in the up-and-out. We won't have anybody else going under the wire for a few hours or days of being human. Everybody will be Other. Nobody will have to cranch, never again. Men can be men. The habermans can be killed decently and properly, the way men were killed in the old days, without anybody keeping them alive. They won't have to work in the up-and-out! There will be no more great pain — think of it! No . . . more . . . great . . . pain! How do we know that Stone is a liar —" Lights began flashing directly into his eyes. (The rudest insult of scanner to scanner was this.)

Vomact again exercised authority. He stepped in front of Parizianski and said something which the others could not see. Parizianski stepped down from the rostrum. Vomact again spoke:

"I think that some of the scanners disagree with our brother Parizianski. I say that the use of the rostrum be suspended till we have had a chance for private discussion. In fifteen minutes I will call the meeting back to order."

Martel looked around for Vomact when the senior had rejoined the group on the floor. Finding the senior, Martel wrote swift script on his tablet, waiting for a chance to thrust the tablet before the senior's eyes. He had written:

Am crnchd. Rspctfly requst prmissn lv now, stnd by ft *orders.D*

Being cranched did strange things to Martel. Most meetings that he attended seemed formal, hearteningly ceremonial, lighting up the dark inward eternities of habermanhood. When he was not cranched, he noticed his body no more than a marble bust notices its marble pedestal. He had stood with them before. He had stood with them effortless hours, while the long-winded ritual broke through the terrible loneliness behind his eyes, and made him feel that the scanners, though a confraternity of the damned, were none the less forever honored by the professional requirements of their mutilation.

This time, it was different. Coming cranched, and in full possession of smell-sound-taste-feeling, he reacted more or less as a normal man would. He saw his friends and colleagues as a lot of cruelly driven ghosts, posturing out the meaningless ritual of their indefeasible damnation. What difference did anything make, once you were a haberman? Why all this talk about habermans and scanners? Habermans were criminals or heretics, and scanners were gentlemen-volunteers, but they were all in the same fix — except that scanners were deemed worthy of the short-time return of the cranching wire, while habermans were simply disconnected while the ships lay in port and were left suspended until they should be awakened, in some hour of emergency or trouble, to work out another spell of their damnation. It was a rare haberman that you saw on the street — someone of special merit or bravery, allowed to look at mankind from the terrible prison of his own mechanified body. And yet, what scanner ever pitied a haberman? What scanner ever honored a haberman except perfunctorily in the line of duty? What had the scanners as a guild and a class ever done for the habermans, except to murder them with a twist of the wrist whenever a haberman, too long beside a scanner, picked up the tricks of the scanning trade and learned how to live at his own will, not the will the scanners imposed? What could the Others, the ordinary men, know of what went on inside the ships? The Others slept in their cylinders, mercifully unconscious until they woke up on whatever other Earth they had consigned themselves to. What could the Others know of the men who had to stay alive within the ship?

What could any Other know of the up-and-out? What Other could look at the biting acid beauty of the stars in open space? What could they tell of the great pain, which started quietly in the marrow, like an ache, and proceeded by the fatigue and nausea of each separate nerve cell, brain cell, touchpoint in the body, until life itself became a terrible aching hunger for silence and for death?

He was a scanner. All right, he *was* a scanner. He had been a scanner from the moment when, wholly normal, he had stood in the sunlight before a subchief of the Instrumentality, and had sworn:

"I pledge my honor and my life to mankind. I sacrificed myself willingly for the welfare of mankind. In accepting the perilous austere honor, I yield all my rights without exception to the honorable chiefs of the Instrumentality and to the honored Confraternity of Scanners."

He had pledged.

He had gone into the haberman device.

He remembered his hell. He had not had such a bad one, even though it had seemed to last a hundred-million years, all of them without sleep. He had learned to feel with his eyes. He had learned to see despite the heavy eyeplates set back of his eyeballs to insulate his eyes from the rest of him. He had learned to watch his skin. He still remembered the time he had noticed dampness on his shirt, and had pulled out his scanning mirror only to discover that he had worn a hole in his side by leaning against a vibrating machine. (A thing like that could not happen to him now; he was too adept at reading his own instruments.) He remembered the way that he had gone up-and-out, and the way that the great pain beat into him, despite the fact that his touch, smell, feeling, and hearing were gone for all ordinary purposes. He remembered killing habermans, and keeping others alive, and standing for months beside the honorable scanner-pilot while neither of them slept. He remembered going ashore on Earth Four, and remembered that he had not enjoyed it, and had realized on that day that there was no reward.

Martel stood among the other scanners. He hated their awkwardness when they moved, their immobility when they stood still. He hated the queer assortment of smells which their bodies yielded unnoticed. He hated the grunts and groans and squawks which they emitted from their deafness. He hated them, and himself.

How could Luci stand him? He had kept his chestbox reading *Danger* for weeks while he courted her, carrying the cranch wire about with him most illegally, and going direct from one cranch to the other without worrying about the fact his indicators all crept up to the edge of *Overload.* He had wooed her without thinking of what would happen if she did say, "Yes." She had.

"And they lived happily ever after." In old books they did, but how could they, in life? He had had eighteen days under the wire in the whole of the past year! Yet she had loved him. She still loved him. He knew it. She fretted about him through the long months that he was in the up-and-out. She tried to make home mean something to him even when he was haberman, make food pretty when it could not be tasted, make herself lovable when she could not be kissed — or might as well not, since a haberman body meant no more than furniture. Luci was patient.

And now, Adam Stone! (He let his tablet fade: how could he leave, now?)

God bless Adam Stone?

Martel could not help feeling a little sorry for himself. No longer would the high keen call of duty carry him through two hundred or so years of the Others' time, two million private eternities of his own. He could slouch and relax. He could forget high space, and let the up-andout be tended by Others. He could cranch as much as he dared. He could be almost normal — almost — for one year or five years or no years. But at least he could stay with Luci. He could go with her into the Wild, where there were Beasts and Old Machines still roving the dark places. Perhaps he would die in the excitement of the hunt, throwing spears at an ancient manshonyagger as it leapt from its lair, or tossing hot spheres at the tribesmen of the Unforgiven who still roamed the Wild. There was still life to live, still a good normal death to die, not the moving of a needle out in the silence and agony of space!

He had been walking about restlessly. His ears were attuned to the sounds of normal speech, so that he did not feel like watching the mouthings of his brethren. Now they seemed to have come to a decision. Vomact was moving to the rostrum. Martel looked about for Chang, and went to stand beside him. Chang whispered.

"You're as restless as water in mid-air! What's the matter? Decranching?"

They both scanned Martel, but the instruments held steady and showed no sign of the cranch giving out.

The great light flared in its call to attention. Again they formed ranks. Vomact thrust his lean old face into the glare, and spoke:

"Scanners and Brothers, I call for a vote." He held himself in the stance which meant: *I am the senior and take command.*

A beltlight flashed in protest.

It was old Henderson. He moved to the rostrum, spoke to Vomact, and — with Vomact's nod of approval — turned full-face to repeat his question:

"Who speaks for the scanners out in space?"

No beltlight or hand answered.

Henderson and Vomact, face to face, conferred for a few moments. Then Henderson faced them again:

"I yield to the senior in command. But I do not yield to a meeting of the Confratemity. There are sixty-eight scanners, and only forty-seven present, of whom one is cranched and U. D. I have therefore proposed that the senior in command assume authority only over an emergency committee of the Confratemity, not over a meeting. Is that agreed and understood by the honorable scanners?"

Hands rose in assent.

Chang murmured in Martel's ear, "Lot of difference that makes! Who can tell the difference between a meeting and a committee?" Martel agreed with the words, but was even more impressed with the way that Chang, while haberman, could control his own voice.

Vomact resumed chairmanship: "We now vote on the question of Adam Stone.

"First, we can assume that he has not succeeded, and that his claims are lies. We know that from our practical experience as scanners. The pain of space is only part of scanning," *(But the essential part, the basis of it all,* thought Martel.) "and we can rest assured that Stone cannot solve the problem of space discipline."

"That tripe again," whispered Chang, unheard save by Martel.

"The space discipline of our confraternity has kept high space clean of war and dispute. Sixty-eight disciplined men control all high space. We are removed by our oath and our haberman status from all Earthly passions.

"Therefore, if Adam Stone has conquered the pain of space, so that Others can wreck our confraternity and bring to space the trouble and ruin which afflicts Earths, I say that Adam Stone is wrong. If Adam Stone succeeds, scanners live in vain!

"Secondly, if Adam Stone has not conquered the pain of space, he will cause great trouble in all the Earths. The Instrumentality and the subchiefs may not give us as many habermans as we need to operate the ships of mankind. There will be wild stories, and fewer recruits, and, worst of all, the discipline of the Confraternity may relax if this kind of nonsensical heresy is spread around.

"Therefore, if Adam Stone has succeeded, he threatens the ruin of the Confraternity and should die.

"I move the death of Adam Stone."

And Vomact made the sign, *The honorable scanners are pleased to vote.*

Martel grabbed wildly for his beltlight. Chang, guessing ahead, had his light out and ready; its bright beam, voting *No,* shone straight up at the ceiling. Martel got his light out and threw its beam upward in dissent. Then he looked around. Out of the forty-seven present, he could see only five or six glittering.

Two more lights went on. Vomact stood as erect as a frozen corpse. Vomact's eyes flashed as he stared back and forth over the group, looking for lights. Several more went on. Finally Vomact took the closing stance:

May it please the scanners to count the vote.

Three of the older men went up on the rostrum with Vomact. They looked over the room. (Martel thought: *These damned ghosts are voting on the life of a real man, a live man! They have no right to do it. I'll tell the Instrumentality!* But he knew that he would not. He thought of Luci and what she might gain by the triumph of Adam Stone: the heart-breaking folly of the vote was then almost too much for Martel to bear.)

All three of the tellers held up their hands in unanimous agreement on the sign of the number: *Fifteen against.*

Vomact dismissed them with a bow of courtesy. He turned and again took the stance: *I am the senior and take command.*

Marveling at his own daring, Martel flashed his beltlight on. He knew that any one of the bystanders might reach over and twist his heartbox to *Overload* for such an act. He felt Chang's hand reaching to catch him by the aircoat. But he eluded Chang's grasp and ran, faster than a scanner should, to the platform. As he ran, he wondered what appeal to make. It was no use talking common sense. Not now. It had to be law.

He jumped up on the rostrum beside Vomact, and took the stance:

Scanners, an Illegality!

He violated good custom while speaking, still in the stance: "A committee has no right to vote death by a majority vote. It takes two-thirds of a full meeting."

He felt Vomact's body lunge behind him, felt himself falling from the rostrum, hitting the floor, hurting his knees and his touch-aware hands. He was helped to his feet. He was scanned. Some scanner he scarcely knew took his instruments and toned him down.

Immediately Martel felt more calm, more detached, and hated himself for feeling so.

He looked up at the rostrum. Vomact maintained the stance signifying: *Order!*

The scanners adjusted their ranks. The two scanners next to Martel took his arms. He shouted at them, but they looked away, and cut themselves off from communication altogether.

Vomact spoke again when he saw the room was quiet: "A scanner came here cranched. Honorable Scanners, I apologize for this. It is not the fault of our great and worthy scanner and friend, Martel. He came here under orders. I told him not to de-cranch. I hoped to spare him an unnecessary haberman. We all know how happily Martel is married, and we wish his brave experiment well. I like Martel. I respect his judgment. I wanted him here. I knew you wanted him here. But he is cranched. He is in no mood to share in the lofty business of the scanners. I therefore propose a solution which will meet all the requirements of fairness. I propose that we rule Scanner Martel out of order for his violation of rules. This violation would be inexcusable if Martel were not cranched.

"But at the same time, in all fairness to Martel, I further propose that we deal with the points raised so improperly by our worthy but disqualified brother."

Vomact gave the sign, *The honorable scanners are pleased to vote.* Martel tried to reach his own beltlight; the dead strong hands held him tightly and he struggled in vain. One lone light shone high: Chang's, no doubt.

Vomact thrust his face into the light again: "Having the approval of our worthy scanners and present company for the general proposal, I now move that this committee declare itself to have the full authority of a meeting, and that this committee further make me responsible for all misdeeds which this committee may enact, to be held answerable before the next full meeting, but not before any other authority beyond the closed and secret ranks of scanners."

Flamboyantly this time, his triumph evident, Vomact assumed the *vote* stance.

Only a few lights shone: far less, patently, than a minority of one-fourth.

Vomact spoke again. The light shone on his high calm forehead, on his dead relaxed cheekbones. His lean cheeks and chin were half-shadowed, save where the lower light picked up and spotlighted his mouth, cruel even in repose. (Vomact was said to be a descendant of some ancient lady who had traversed, in an illegitimate and inexplicable fashion, some hundreds of years of time in a single night. Her name, the Lady Vomact, had passed into legend; but her blood and her archaic lust for mastery lived on in the mute masterful body of her descendant. Martel could believe the old tales as he stared at the rostrum, wondering what untraceable mutation had left the Vomact kin as predators among mankind.) Calling loudly with the movement of his lips, but still without sound, Vomact appealed:

"The honorable committee is now pleased to reaffirm the sentence of death issued against the heretic and enemy, Adam Stone." Again the *vote* stance.

Again Chang's light shone lonely in its isolated protest.

Vomact then made his final move:

"I call for the designation of the senior scanner present as the manager of the sentence. I call for authorization to him to appoint executioners, one or many, who shall make evident the will and majesty of scanners. I ask that I be accountable for the deed, and not for the means. The deed is a noble deed, for the protection of mankind and for the honor of the scanners; but of the means it must be said that they are to be the best at hand, and no more. Who knows the true way to kill an Other, here on a crowded and watchful Earth? This is no mere matter of discharging a cylindered sleeper, no mere question of upgrading the needle of a haberman. When people die down here, it is not like the up-and-out. They die reluctantly. Killing within the Earth is not our usual business, 0 Brothers and Scanners, as you know well. You must choose me to choose my agent as I see fit. Otherwise the common knowledge will become the common betrayal whereas if I alone know the responsibility, I alone could betray us, and you will not have far to look in case the Instrumentality comes searching." *(What about the killer you choose?* thought Martel. *He too will know unless — unless you silence him forever.)*

Vomact went into the stance: *The honorable scanners are pleased to vote.*

One light of protest shone; Chang's, again.

Martel imagined that he could see a cruel joyful smile on Vomact's dead face — the smile of a man who knew himself righteous and who found his righteousness upheld and affirmed by militant authority.

Martel tried one last time to come free.

The dead hands held. They were locked like vises until their owners' eyes unlocked them: how else could they hold the piloting month by month?

Martel then shouted: "Honorable Scanners, this is judicial murder."

No ear heard him. He was cranched, and alone.

Nonetheless, he shouted again: "You endanger the Confraternity."

Nothing happened.

The echo of his voice sounded from one end of the room to the other. No head turned. No eyes met his.

Martel realized that as they paired for talk, the eyes of the scanners avoided him. He saw that no one desired to watch his speech. He knew that behind the cold faces of his friends there lay compassion or amusement. He knew that they knew him to be cranched — absurd, normal, manlike, temporarily no scanner. But he knew that in this matter the wisdom of scanners was nothing. He knew that only a cranched scanner could feel with his very blood the outrage and anger which deliberate murder would provoke among the Others. He knew that the Confraternity endangered itself, and knew that the most ancient prerogative of law was the monopoly of death. Even the ancient nations, in the times of the Wars, before the Beasts, before men went into the up-and-out — even the ancients had known this. How did they say it? *Only the state shall kill.* The states were gone but the Instrumentality remained, and the Instrumentality could not pardon things which occurred within the Earths but beyond its authority. Death in space was the business, the right of the scanners: how could the Instrumentality enforce its laws in a place where all men who wakened, wakened only to die in the great pain? Wisely did the Instrumentality leave space to the scanners, wisely had the Confraternity not meddled inside the Earths. *And* now the Confraternity itself was going to step forth as an outlaw band, as a gang of rogues as stupid and reckless as the tribes of the Unforgiven!

Martel knew this because he was cranched. Had he been haberman, he would have thought only with his mind, not with his heart and guts and blood. How could the other scanners know?

Vomact returned for the last time to the rostrum: *The committee has met and its will shall be done.* Verbally he added: "Senior among you, I ask your loyalty and your silence."

At that point, the two scanners let his arms go. Martel rubbed his numb hands, shaking his fingers to get the circulation back into the cold fingertips. With real freedom, he began to think of what he might still do. He scanned himself: the cranching held. He might have a day. Well, he could go on even if haberman, but it would be inconvenient, having to talk with finger and tablet. He looked about for Chang. He saw his friend standing patient and immobile in a quiet corner. Martel moved slowly, so as not to attract any more attention to himself than could be helped. He faced Chang, moved until his face was in the light, and then articulated:

"What are we going to do? You're not going to let them kill Adam Stone, are you? Don't you realize what Stone's work will mean to us, if it succeeds? No more scanners. No more habermans. No more pain in the up-and-out. I tell you, if the others were all cranched, as I am, they would see it in a human way, not with the narrow crazy logic which they used in the meeting. We've got to stop them. How can we do it? What are we going to do? What does Parizianski think? Who has been chosen?"

"Which question do you want me to answer?"

Martel laughed. (It felt good to laugh, even then; it felt like being a man.) "Will you help me?"

Chang's eyes flashed across Martel's face as Chang answered: "No. No. No."

"You won't help?"

"Why not, Chang? Why not?"

"I am a scanner. The vote has been taken. You would do the same if you were not in this unusual condition."

"I'm not in an unusual condition. I'm cranched. That merely means that I see things the way that the Others would. I see the stupidity. The recklessness. The selfishness. It is murder."

"What is murder? Have you not killed? You are not one of the Others. You are a scanner. You will be sorry for what you are about to do, if you do not watch out."

"But why did you vote against Vomact then? Didn't you too see what Adam Stone means to all of us? Scanners will live in vain. Thank God for that! Can't you see it?"

"No."

"But you talk to me, Chang. You are my friend?"

"I talk to you. I am your friend. Why not?"

"But what are you going to do?"

"Nothing, Martel. Nothing."

"Will you help me?"

"Not even to save Stone?"

"Then I will go to Parizianski for help."

"It will do you no good."

"Why not? He's more human than you, right now."

"He will not help you, because he has the job. Vomact designated him to kill Adam Stone."

Martel stopped speaking in mid-movement. He suddenly took the stance: *I thank you, Brother, and I depart.*

At the window he turned and faced the room. He saw that Vomact's eyes were upon him. He gave the stance, *I thank you, Brother, and I depart,* and added the flourish of respect which is shown when seniors are present. Vomact caught the sign, and Martel could see the cruel lips move. He thought he saw the words ". . . take good care of yourself. . ." but did not wait to inquire. He stepped backward and dropped out the window.

Once below the window and out of sight, he adjusted his air-coat to a maximum speed. He swam lazily in the air, scanning himself thoroughly, and adjusting his adrenal intake down. He then made the movement of release, and felt the cold air rush past his face like run-fling water.

Adam Stone had to be at Chief Downport.

Adam Stone had to be there.

Wouldn't Adam Stone be surprised in the night? Surprised to meet the strangest of beings, the first renegade among scanners. (Martel suddenly appreciated that it was of himself he was thinking. Martel the Traitor to Scanners! That sounded strange and bad. But what of Martel, the Loyal to Mankind? Was that not compensation? And if he won, he won Luci. If he lost, he lost nothing — an unconsidered and expendable haberman. It happened to be himself. But in contrast to the immense reward, to mankind, to the Confraternity, to Luci, what did that matter?)

Martel thought to himself: "Adam Stone will have two visitors tonight. Two scanners, who are the friends of one another." He hoped that Parizianski was still his friend.

"And the world," he added, "depends on which of us gets there first." Multifaceted in their brightness, the lights of Chief Downport began to shine through the mist ahead. Martel could see the outer towers of the city and glimpsed the phosphorescent periphery which kept back the Wild, whether Beasts, Machines, or the Unforgiven.

Once more Martel invoked the lords of his chance: "Help me to pass for an Other!"

Within the Downport, Martel had less trouble than he thought. He draped his aircoat over his shoulder so that it concealed the instruments. He took up his scanning mirror, and made up his face from the inside, by adding tone and animation to his blood and nerves until the muscles of his face glowed and the skin gave out a healthy sweat. That way he looked like an ordinary man who had just completed a long night flight.

After straightening out his clothing, and hiding his tablet within his jacket, he faced the problem of what to do about the talking finger. If he kept the nail, it would show him to be a scanner. He would be respected, but he would be identified. He might be stopped by the guards whom the Instrumentality had undoubtedly set around the person of Adam Stone. If he broke the nail — But he couldn't! No scanner in the history of the Confraternity had ever willingly broken his nail. That would be resignation, and there was no such thing. The only way *out*, was in the up-and-out! Martel put his finger to his mouth and bit off the nail. He looked at the now-queer finger, and sighed to himself.

He stepped toward the city gate, slipping his hand into his jacket and running up his muscular strength to four times normal.

He started to scan, and then realized that his instruments were masked. *Might as well take all the chances at once,* he thought.

The watcher stopped him with a searching wire. The sphere thumped suddenly against Martel's chest.

"Are you a man?" said the unseen voice. (Martel knew that as a scanner in haberman condition, his own field-charge would have illuminated the sphere.)

"I am a man." Martel knew that the timbre of his voice had been good; he hoped that it would not be taken for that of a man-shonyagger or a Beast or an Unforgiven one, who with mimicry sought to enter the cities and ports of mankind.

"Name, number, rank, purpose, function, time departed."

"Martel." He had to remember his old number, not Scanner 34. "Sunward **4234**, 782nd Year of Space. Rank, rising subchief." That was no lie, but his substantive rank. "Purpose, personal and lawful within the limits of this city. No function of the Instrumentality. Departed Chief Outpost **2019** hours." Everything now depended on whether he was believed, or would be checked against Chief Outpost.

The voice was fiat and routine: "Time desired within the city." Martel used the standard phrase: "Your honorable sufferance is requested."

He stood in the cool night air, waiting. Far above him, through a gap in the mist, he could see the poisonous glittering in the sky of scanners. *The stars are my enemies,* he thought: *I have mastered the stars but they hate me. Ho, that sounds ancient! Like ci book. Too much cranching.*

The voice returned: "Sunward **4234** dash **782** rising subchief Mar-tel, enter the lawful gates of the city. Welcome. Do you desire food, raiment, money, or companionship?" The voice had no hospitality in it, just business. This was certainly different from entering a city in a scanner's role! Then the petty officers came out, and threw their belt-lights on their fretful faces, and mouthed their words with preposterous deference, shouting against the stone deafness of scanner's ears. So that was the way that a sub-chief was treated: matter of fact, but not bad. Not bad.

Martel replied: "I have that which I need, but beg of the city a favor. My friend Adam Stone is here. I desire to see him, on urgent and personal lawful affairs."

The voice replied: "Did you have an appointment with Adam Stone?"

"The city will find him. What is his number?"

"I have forgotten it."

"You have forgotten it? Is not Adam Stone a magnate of the Instrumentality? Are you truly his friend?"

"Truly." Martel let a little annoyance creep into his voice. "Watcher, doubt me and call your subchief."

"No doubt implied. Why do you not know the number? This must go into the record," added the voice.

"We were friends in childhood. He has crossed the —" Martel started to say "the up-and-out" and remembered that the phrase was current only among scanners. "He has leapt from Earth to Earth, and has just now returned. I knew him well and I seek him out. I have word of his kith. May the Instrumentality protect us!"

"Heard and believed. Adam Stone will be searched."

At a risk, though a slight one, of having the sphere sound an alarm for *nonhuman,* Martel cut in on his scanner speaker within his jacket. He saw the trembling needle of light await his words and he started to write on it with his blunt finger. *That won't work,* he thought, and had a moment's panic until he found his comb, which had a sharp enough tooth to write. He wrote: "Emergency none. Martel Scanner calling Parizianski Scanner."

The needle quivered and the reply glowed and faded out: "Parizianski Scanner on duty and D. C. Calls taken by Scanner Relay."

Martel cut off his speaker.

Parizianski was somewhere around. Could he have crossed the direct way, right over the city wall, setting off the alert, and invoking official business when the petty officers overtook him in midair? Scarcely. That meant that a number of other scanners must have come in with Parizianski, all of them pretending to be in search of a few of the tenuous pleasures which could be enjoyed by a haberman, such as the sight of the newspictures or the viewing of beautiful women in the Pleasure Gallery. Parizianski was around, but he could not have moved privately, because Scanner Central registered him on duty and recorded his movements city by city.

The voice returned. Puzzlement was expressed in it. "Adam Stone is found and awakened. He has asked pardon of the Honorable, and says he knows no Martel. Will you see Adam Stone in the morning? The city will bid you welcome."

Martel ran out of resources. It was hard enough mimicking a man without having to tell lies in the guise of one. Martel could only repeat:

"Tell him I am Martel. The husband of Luci."

"It will be done."

Again the silence, and the hostile stars, and the sense that Parizianski was somewhere near and getting nearer; Martel felt his heart beating faster. He stole a glimpse at his chestbox and set his heart down a point. He felt calmer, even though he had not been able to scan with care.

The voice this time was cheerful, as though an annoyance had been settled: "Adam Stone consents to see you. Enter Chief Downport, and welcome."

The little sphere dropped noiselessly to the ground and the wire whispered away into the darkness. A bright arc of narrow light rose from the ground in front of Martel and swept through the city to one of the higher towers — apparently a hostel, which Martel had never entered. Martel plucked his aircoat to his chest for ballast, stepped heel-and-toe on the beam, and felt himself whistle through the air to an entrance window which sprang up before him as suddenly as a devouring mouth.

A tower guard stood in the doorway. "You are awaited, sir. Do you bear weapons, sir?"

"None," said Martel, grateful that he was relying on his own strength.

The guard led him past the check-screen. Martel noticed the quick flight of a warning across the screen as his instruments registered and identified him as a scanner. But the guard had not noticed it.

The guard stopped at a door. "Adam Stone is armed. He is lawfully armed by authority of the Instrumentality and by the liberty of this city. All those who enter are given warning."

Martel nodded in understanding at the man and went in.

Adam Stone was a short man, stout and benign. His gray hair rose stiffly from a low forehead. His whole face was red and merry-looking. He looked like a jolly guide from the Pleasure Gallery, not like a man who had been at the edge of the up-and-out, fighting the great pain without haberman protection.

He stared at Martel. His look was puzzled, perhaps a little annoyed, but not hostile.

Martel came to the point. "You do not know me. I lied. My name is Martel, and I mean you no harm. But I lied. I beg the honorable gift of your hospitality. Remain armed. Direct your weapon against me —"

Stone smiled: "I am doing so," and Martel noticed the small wire-point in Stone's capable, plump hand.

"Good. Keep on guard against me. It will give you confidence in what I shall say. But do, I beg you, give us a screen of privacy. I want no casual lookers. This is a matter of life and death."

"First: whose life and death?" Stone's face remained calm, his voice even.

"Yours, and mine, and the worlds'."

"You are cryptic but I agree." Stone called through the doorway:

"Privacy please." There was a sudden hum, and all the little noises of the night quickly vanished from the air of the room.

Said Adam Stone: "Sir, who are you? What brings you here?"

"I am Scanner 34."

"You a scanner? I don't believe it."

For answer, Martel pulled his jacket open, showing his chestbox. Stone looked up at him, amazed. Martel explained:

"I am cranched. Have you never seen it before?"

"Not with men. On animals. Amazing! But — what do you want?"

"The truth. Do you fear me?"

"Not with this," said Stone, grasping the wirepoint. "But I shall tell you the truth."

"Is it true that you have conquered the great pain?"

Stone hesitated, seeking words for an answer.

"Quick, can you tell me how you have done it, so that I may believe you?"

"I have loaded the ships with life."

"Life?"

"Life. I don't know what the great pain is, but I did find that in the experiments, when I sent out masses of animals or plants, the life in the center of the mass lived longest. I built ships — small ones, of course — and sent them out with rabbits, with monkeys —"

"Those are Beasts?"

"Yes. With small Beasts. And the Beasts came back unhurt. They came back because the walls of the ships were filled with life. I tried many kinds, and finally found a sort of life which lives in the waters. Oysters. Oyster-beds. The outermost oysters died in the great pain. The inner ones lived. The passengers were unhurt."

"But they were Beasts?"

"Not only Beasts. Myself."

"You!"

"I came through space alone. Through what you call the up-and-out, alone. Awake and sleeping. I am unhurt. If you do not believe me, ask your brother scanners. Come and see my ship in the morning. I will be glad to see you then, along with your brother scanners. I am going to demonstrate before the chiefs of the Instrumentality."

Martel repeated his question: "You came here alone?"

Adam Stone grew testy: "Yes, alone. Go back and check your scanner's register if you do not believe me. You never put me in a bottle to cross Space."

Martel's face was radiant. "I believe you now. It is true. No more scanners. No more habermans. No more cranching."

Stone looked significantly toward the door.

Martel did not take the hint. "I must tell you that —"

"Sir, tell me in the morning. Go enjoy your cranch. Isn't it supposed to be pleasure? Medically I know it well. But not in practice."

"It is pleasure. It's normality — for a while. But listen. The scanners have sworn to destroy you, and your work."

"What!"

"They have met and have voted and sworn. You will make scanners unnecessary, they say. You will bring the ancient wars back to the world, if scanning is lost and the scanners live in vain!"

Adam Stone was nervous but kept his wits about him: "You're a scanner. Are you going to kill me — or try?"

"No, you fool. I have betrayed the Confraternity. Call guards the moment I escape. Keep guards around you. I will try to intercept the killer."

Martel saw a blur in the window. Before Stone could turn, the wirepoint was whipped out of his hand. The blur solidified and took form as Parizianski.

Martel recognized what Parizianski was doing: *High speed.* Without thinking of his cranch, he thrust his hand to his chest, set himself up to *High speed* too. Waves of fire, like the great pain, but hotter, flooded over him. He fought to keep his face readable as he stepped in front of Parizianski and gave the sign,

Top emergency.

Parizianski spoke, while the normally moving body of Stone stepped away from them as slowly as a drifting cloud: "Get out of my way. I am on a mission."

"I know it. I stop you here and now. Stop. Stop. Stop. Stone is right."

Parizianski's lips were barely readable in the haze of pain which flooded Martel. (He thought: *God, God, God of the ancients! Let me hold on! Let me live under* Overload *just long enough!)* Parizianski was saying: "Get out of my way. By order of the Confraternity, get out of my way!" And Parizianski gave the sign, *Help I demand in the name of my duty!*

Martel choked for breath in the syrup-like air. He tried one last time:

"Parizianski, friend, my friend. Stop. Stop." (No scanner had ever murdered scanner before.)

Parizianski made the sign: *You are unfit for duty, and I will take over.*

Martel thought, *For the first time in the world!* as he reached over and twisted Parizianski's brainbox up to *Overload.* Parizianski's eyes glittered in terror and understanding. His body began to drift down toward the floor.

Martel had just strength to reach his own chestbox. As he faded into haberman or death, he knew not which, he felt his fingers turning on the control of speed, turning down. He tried to speak, to say, "Get a scanner, I need help, get a scanner . . ."

But the darkness rose about him, and the numb silence clasped him.

Martel awakened to see the face of Luci near his own.

He opened his eyes wider, and found that he was hearing — hearing the sound of her happy weeping, the sound of her chest as she caught the air back into her throat.

He spoke weakly: "Still cranched? Alive?"

Another face swam into the blur beside Luci's. It was Adam Stone. His deep voice rang across immensities of space before coming to Martel's hearing. Martel tried to read Stone's lips, but could not make them out. He went back to listening to the voice:

"— not cranched. Do you understand me? NOT cranched!"

Martel tried to say: "But I can hear! I can feel!" The others got his sense if not his words.

Adam Stone spoke again:

"You have gone back through the haberman. I put you back first. I didn't know how it would work in practice, but I had the theory all worked out. You don't think the Instrumentality would waste the scanners, do you? You go back to normality. We are letting the habermans die as fast as the ships come in. They don't need to live any more. But we are restoring the scanners. You are the first. Do you understand? You are the first. Take it easy, now."

Adam Stone smiled. Dimly behind Stone, Martel thought that he saw the face of one of the chiefs of the Instrumentality. That face, too, smiled at him, and then both faces disappeared upward and away.

Martel tried to lift his head, to scan himself. He could not. Luci stared at him, calming herself, but with an expression of loving perplexity. She said,

"My darling husband! You're back again, to stay!"

Still, Martel tried to see his box. Finally he swept his hand across his chest with a clumsy motion. There was nothing there. The instruments were gone. He was back to normality but still alive.

In the deep weak peacefulness of his mind, another troubling thought took shape. He tried to write with his finger, the way that Luci wanted him to, but he had neither pointed fingernail nor scanner's tablet. He had to use his voice. He summoned up his strength and whispered:

"Scanners?"

"Yes, darling? What is it?"

"Scanners?"

"Scanners. Oh, yes, darling, they're all right. They had to arrest some of them for going into *High speed* and running away. But the Instrumentality caught them all — all those on the ground — and they're happy now. Do you know, darling," she laughed, "some of them didn't want to be restored to normality. But Stone and the chiefs persuaded them."

"Vomact?"

"He's fine, too. He's staying cranched until he can be restored. Do you know, he has arranged for scanners to take new jobs. You're all to be deputy chiefs for Space. Isn't that nice? But he got himself made chief for Space. You're all going to be pilots, so that your fraternity and guild can go on. And Chang's getting changed right now. You'll see him soon."

Her face turned sad. She looked at him earnestly and said: "I might as well tell you now. You'll worry otherwise. There has been one accident. Only one. When you and your friend called on Adam Stone, your friend was so happy that he forgot to scan, and he let himself die of *Overload.*"

"Called on Stone?"

"Yes. Don't you remember? Your friend."

He still looked surprised, so she said:

"Parizianski."

THE GAME OF RAT AND DRAGON

1. THE TABLE

Pinlighting is a hell of a way to earn a living. Underhill was furious as he closed the door behind himself. It didn't make much sense to wear a uniform and look like a soldier if people didn't appreciate what you did.

He sat down in his chair, laid his head back in the headrest, and pulled the helmet down over his forehead.

As he waited for the pin-set to warm up, he remembered the girl in the outer corridor. She had looked at it, then looked at him scornfully.

"Meow." That was all she had said. Yet it had cut him like a knife.

What did she think he was — a fool, a loafer, a uniformed nonentity? Didn't she know that for every half-hour of pinlighting, he got a minimum of two month's recuperation in the hospital?

By now the set was warm. He felt the squares of space around him, sensed himself at the middle of an immense grid, a cubic grid, full of nothing. Out in that nothingness, he could sense the hollow aching horror of space itself and could feel the terrible anxiety which his mind encountered whenever it met the faintest trace of inert dust.

As he relaxed, the comforting solidity of the Sun, the clockwork of the familiar planets and the moon rang in on him. Our own solar system was as charming and as simple as an ancient cuckoo clock filled with familiar ticking and with reassuring noises. The odd little moons of Mars swung around their planet like frantic mice, yet their regularity was itself an assurance that all was well. Far above the plane of the ecliptic, he could feel half a ton of dust more or less drifting outside the lanes of human travel.

Here there was nothing to fight, nothing to challenge the mind, to tear the living soul out of a body with its roots dripping in effluvium as tangible as blood.

Nothing ever moved in on the solar system. He could wear the pinset forever and be nothing more than a sort of telepathic astronomer, a man who could feel the hot, warm protection of the sun throbbing and burning against his living mind.

Woodley came in.

"Same old ticking world," said Underhill. "Nothing to report. No wonder they didn't develop the pin-set until they began to planoform. Down here with the hot sun around us, it feels so good and so quiet. You can feel everything spinning and turning. It's nice and sharp and compact. It's sort of like sitting around home."

Woodley grunted. He was not much given to flights of fantasy.

Undeterred, Underhill went on, "It must have been pretty good to have been an ancient man. I wonder why they burned up their world with war. They didn't have to planoform. They didn't have to go out to earn their livings among the stars. They didn't have to dodge the rats or play the game. They couldn't have invented pinlighting because they didn't have any need of it, did they, Woodley?"

Woodley grunted, "Uh-huh." Woodley was twenty-six years old and due to retire in one more year. He already had a farm picked out. He had gotten through ten years of hard work pinlighting with the best of them. He had kept his sanity by not thinking very much about his job, meeting the strains of the task whenever he had to meet them and thinking nothing more about his duties until the next emergency arose.

Woodley never made a point of getting popular among the partners. None of the partners liked him very much. Some of them even resented him. He was suspected of thinking ugly thoughts of the partners on occasion, but since none of the partners ever thought a complaint in articulate form, the other pinlighters and the chiefs of the Instrumentality left him alone.

Underhill was still full of the wonder of their job. Happily he babbled on, "What does happen to us when we planoform? Do you think it's sort of like dying? Did you ever see anybody who had his soul pulled out?"

"Pulling souls is just a way of talking about it," said Woodley. "After all these years, nobody knows whether we have souls or not"

"But I saw one once. I saw what Dogwood looked like when he came apart. There was something funny. It looked wet and sort of sticky as if it were bleeding and it went out of him — and you know what they did to Dogwood? They took him away, up in that part of the hospital where you and I never go — way up at the top part where the others are, where the others always have to go if they are alive after the rats of the up-and-out have gotten them."

Woodley sat down and lit an ancient pipe. He was burning something called tobacco in it. It was a dirty sort of habit, but it made him look very dashing and adventurous.

"Look here, youngster. You don't have to worry about that stuff. Pin-lighting is getting better all the time. The partners are getting better. I've seen them pinlight two rats forty-six million miles apart in one and a half milliseconds. As long as people had to try to work the pin-sets themselves, there was always the chance that with a minimum of four-hundred milliseconds for the human mind to set a pinlight, we wouldn't light the rats up fast enough to protect our planoforming ships. The partners have changed all that. Once they get going, they're faster than rats. And they always will be. I know it's not easy, letting a partner share your mind —"

"It's not easy for them, either," said Underhill. "Don't worry about them. They're not human. Let them take care of themselves. I've seen more pinlighters go crazy from monkeying around with partners than I have ever seen caught by the rats. How many of them do you actually know of that got grabbed by rats?"

Underhill looked down at his fingers, which shone green and purple in the vivid light thrown by the tuned-in pin-set, and counted ships. The thumb for the *Andromeda,* lost with crew and passengers, the index finger and the middle finger for *Release Ships 43* and *56,* found with their pin-sets burned out and every man, woman, and child on board dead or insane. The ring finger, the little finger, and the thumb of the other hand were the first three battleships to be lost to the rats — lost as people realized that there was something out there underneath space itself which was alive, capricious, and malevolent.

Planoforming was sort of funny. It felt like . . . like nothing much. Like the twinge of a mild electric shock.

Like the ache of a sore tooth bitten on for the first time.

Like a slightly painful flash of light against the eyes.

Yet in that time, a forty-thousand-ton ship lifting free above Earth disappeared somehow or other into two dimensions and appeared half a lightyear or fifty lightyears off.

At one moment, he would be sitting in the Fighting Room, the pin-set ready and the familiar solar system ticking around inside his head. For a second or a year (he could never tell how long it really was, subjectively), the funny little flash went through him and then he was loose in the up-and-out, the terrible open spaces between the stars, where the stars themselves felt like pimples on his telepathic mind and the planets were too far away to be sensed or read.

Somewhere in this outer space, a gruesome death awaited, death and horror of a kind which man had never encountered until he reached out for interstellar space itself. Apparently the light of the suns kept the dragons away.

Dragons. That was what people called them. To ordinary people, there was nothing, nothing except the shiver of planoforming and the hammer blow of sudden death or the dark spastic note of lunacy descending into their minds.

But to the telepaths, they were dragons.

In the fraction of a second between the telepaths' awareness of a hostile something out in the black, hollow nothingness of space and the impact of a ferocious, ruinous psychic blow against all living things within the ship, the telepaths had sensed entities something like the dragons of ancient human lore, beasts more clever than beasts, demons more tangible than demons, hungry vortices of aliveness and hate compounded by unknown means out of the thin, tenuous matter between the stars.

It took a surviving ship to bring back the news — a ship in which, by sheer chance, a telepath had a light-beam ready, turning it out at the innocent dust so that, within the panorama of his mind, the dragon dissolved into nothing at all and the other passengers, themselves non-telepathic, went about their way not realizing that their own immediate deaths had been averted.

From then on, it was easy — almost.

Planoforming ships always carried telepaths. Telepaths had their sensitiveness enlarged to an immense range by the pin-sets, which were telepathic amplifiers adapted to the mammal mind. The pin-sets in turn were electronically geared into small dirigible light bombs. Light did it.

Light broke up the dragons, allowed the ships to reform three-dimensionally, skip, skip, skip, as they moved from star to star.

The odds suddenly moved down from a hundred to one against mankind to sixty to forty in mankind's favor.

This was not enough. The telepaths were trained to become ultrasensitive, trained to become aware of the dragons in less than a millisecond.

But it was found that the dragons could move a million miles in just under two milliseconds and that this was not enough for the human mind to activate the light beams.

Attempts had been made to sheath the ships in light at all times.

This defense wore out.

As mankind learned about the dragons, so too, apparently, the dragons learned about mankind. Somehow they flattened their own bulk and came in on extremely flat trajectories very quickly.

Intense light was needed, light of sunlike intensity. This could be provided only by light bombs. Pinlighting came into existence.

Pinlighting consisted of the detonation of ultra-vivid miniature photonuclear bombs, which converted a few ounces of a magnesium isotope into pure visible radiance.

The odds kept coming down in mankind's favor, yet ships were being lost.

It became so bad that people didn't even want to find the ships because the rescuers knew what they would see. It was sad to bring back to Earth three hundred bodies ready for burial and two hundred or three hundred lunatics, damaged beyond repair, to be wakened, and fed, and cleaned, and put to sleep, wakened and fed again until their lives were ended.

Telepaths tried to reach into the minds of the psychotics who had been damaged by the dragons, but they found nothing there beyond vivid spouting columns of fiery terror bursting from the primordial id itself, the volcanic source of life.

Then came the partners.

Man and partner could do together what man could not do alone. Men had the intellect. Partners had the speed.

The partners rode their tiny craft, no larger than footballs, outside the spaceships. They planoformed with the ships. They rode beside them in their six-pound craft ready to attack.

The tiny ships of the partners were swift. Each carried a dozen pinlights, bombs no bigger than thimbles.

The pinlighters threw the partners — quite literally threw — by means of mind-to-firing relays directly at the dragons.

What seemed to be dragons to the human mind appeared in the form of gigantic rats in the minds of the partners.

Out in the pitiless nothingness of space, the partners' minds responded to an instinct as old as life. The partners attacked, striking with a speed faster than man's, going from attack to attack until the rats or themselves were destroyed. Almost all the time it was the partners who won.

With the safety of the interstellar skip, skip, skip of the ships, commerce increased immensely, the population of all the colonies went up, and the demand for trained partners increased.

Underhill and Woodley were a part of the third generation of pinlighters; and yet, to them, it seemed as though their craft had endured forever.

Gearing space into minds by means of the pin-set, adding the partners to those minds, keying up the minds for the tension of a fight on which all depended — this was more than human synapses could stand for long. Underhill needed his two months rest after half an hour of fighting. Woodley needed his retirement after ten years of service. They were young. They were good. But they had limitations.

So much depended on the choice of partners, so much on the sheer luck of who drew whom.

2. THE SHUFFLE

Father Moontree and the little girl named West entered the room. They were the other two pinlighters. The human complement of the Fighting Room was now complete.

Father Moontree was a red-faced man of forty-five who had lived the peaceful life of a farmer until he reached his fortieth year. Only then, belatedly, did the authorities find he was telepathic and agree to let him, late in life, enter upon the career of pinlighter. He did well at it, but he was fantastically old for this kind of business.

Father Moontree looked at the glum Woodley and the musing Underhill. "How're the youngsters today? Ready for a good fight?"

"Father always wants a fight," giggled the little girl named West. She was such a little little girl. Her giggle was high and childish. She looked like the last person in the world one would expect to find in the rough, sharp dueling of pinlighting.

Underhill had been amused one time when he found one of the most sluggish of the partners coming away happy from contact with the mind of the girl named West.

Usually the partners didn't care much about the human minds with which they were paired for the journey. The partners seemed to take the attitude that human minds were complex and fouled up beyond belief, anyhow. No partner ever questioned the superiority of the human mind, though very few of the partners were much impressed by that superiority.

The partners liked people. They were willing to fight with them. They were even willing to die for them. But when a partner liked an individual the way, for example, that Captain Wow or the Lady May liked Underhill, the liking had nothing to do with intellect. It was a matter of temperament, of feel.

Underhill knew perfectly well that Captain Wow regarded his, Underhills, brains as silly. What Captain Wow liked was Underhill's friendly emotional structure, the cheerfulness and glint of wicked amusement that shot through Underhill's unconscious thought patterns, and the gaiety with which Underhill faced danger. The words, the history books, the ideas, the science — Underhill could sense all that in his own mind, reflected back from Captain Wow's mind, as so much rubbish.

Miss West looked at Underhill. "I bet you've put stickum on the stones."

"I did not!"

Underhill felt his ears grow red with embarrassment. During his novitiate, he had tried to cheat in the lottery because he got particularly fond of a special partner, a lovely young mother named Murr. It was so much easier to operate with Murr and she was so affectionate toward him that he forgot pinlighting was hard work and that he was not instructed to have a good time with his partner. They were both designed and prepared to go into deadly battle together.

One cheating had been enough. They had found him out and he had been laughed at for years.

Father Moontree picked up the imitation-leather cup and shook the stone dice which assigned them their partners for the trip. By senior rights he took first draw.

He grimaced. He had drawn a greedy old character, a tough old male whose mind was full of slobbering thoughts of food, veritable oceans full of half spoiled fish. Father Moontree had once said that he burped cod liver oil for weeks after drawing that particular glutton, so strongly had the telepathic image of fish impressed itself upon his mind. Yet the glutton was a glutton for danger as well as for fish. He had killed sixty-three dragons, more than any other partner in the service, and was quite literally worth his weight in gold.

The little girl West came next. She drew Captain Wow. When she saw who it was, she smiled.

"I like him," she said. "He's such fun to fight with. He feels so nice and cuddly in my mind."

"Cuddly, hell," said Woodley. "I've been in his mind, too. It's the most leering mind in this ship, bar none."

"Nasty man," said the little girl. She said it declaratively, without reproach.

Underhill, looking at her, shivered.

He didn't see how she could take Captain Wow so calmly. Captain Wow's mind did leer. When Captain Wow got excited in the middle of a battle, confused images of dragons, deadly rats, luscious beds, the smell of fish, and the shock of space all scrambled together in his mind as he and Captain Wow, their consciousnesses linked together through the pin-set, became a fantastic composite of human being and Persian cat.

That's the trouble with working with cats, thought Underhill. It's a pity that nothing else anywhere will serve as partner. Cats were all right once you got in touch with them telepathically. They were smart enough to meet the needs of the fight, but their motives and desires were certainly different from those of humans.

They were companionable enough as long as you thought tangible images at them, but their minds just closed up and went to sleep when you recited Shakespeare or Colegrove, or if you tried to tell them what space was.

It was sort of funny realizing that the partners who were so grim and mature out here in space were the same cute little animals that people had used as pets for thousands of years back on Earth. He had embarrassed himself more than once while on the ground saluting perfectly ordinary non-telepathic cats because he had forgotten for the moment that they were not partners.

He picked up the cup and shook out his stone dice.

He was lucky — he drew the Lady May.

The Lady May was the most thoughtful partner he had ever met. In her, the finely bred pedigree mind of a Persian cat had reached one of its highest peaks of development. She was more complex than any human woman, but the complexity was all one of emotions, memory, hope, and discriminated experience — experience sorted through without benefit of words.

When he had first come into contact with her mind, he was astonished at its clarity. With her he remembered her kittenhood. He remembered every mating experience she had ever had. He saw in a half recognizable gallery all the other pinlighters with whom she had been paired for the fight. And he saw himself radiant, cheerful, and desirable.

He even thought he caught the edge of a longing —

A very flattering and yearning thought: *What a pity he is not a cat.*

Woodley picked up the last stone. He drew what he deserved — a sullen, scarred old tomcat with none of the verve of Captain Wow. Woodley's partner was the most animal of all the cats on the ship, a low, brutish type with a dull mind. Even telepathy had not refined his character. His ears were half chewed off from the first fights in which he had engaged. He was a serviceable fighter, nothing more.

Woodley grunted.

Underhill glanced at him oddly. Didn't Woodley ever do anything but grunt?

Father Moontree looked at the other three. "You might as well get your partners now. I'll let the scanner know were ready to go into the up-and-out."

3. THE DEAL

Underhill spun the combination lock on the Lady May's cage. He woke her gently and took her into his arms. She humped her back luxuriously, stretched her claws, started to purr, thought better of it, and licked him on the wrist instead. He did not have the pin-set on, so their minds were closed to each other, but in the angle of her mustache and in the movement of her ears, he caught some sense of the gratification she experienced in finding him as her partner.

He talked to her in human speech, even though speech meant nothing to a cat when the pin-set was not on.

"It's a damn shame, sending a sweet little thing like you whirling around in the coldness of nothing to hunt for rats that are bigger and deadlier than all of us put together. You didn't ask for this kind of fight, did you?"

For answer, she licked his hand, purred, tickled his cheek with her long fluffy tail, turned around and faced him, golden eyes shining.

For a moment, they stared at each other, man squatting, cat standing erect on her hind legs, front claws digging into his knee. Human eyes and cat eyes looked across an immensity which no words could meet, but which affection spanned in a single glance.

"Time to get in," he said.

She walked docilely to her spheroid carrier. She climbed in. He saw to it that her miniature pin-set rested firmly and comfortably against the base of her brain. He made sure that her claws were padded so that she could not tear herself in the excitement of battle.

Softly he said to her, "Ready?"

For answer, she preened her back as much as her harness would permit and purred softly within the confines of the frame that held her.

He slapped down the lid and watched the sealant ooze around the seam. For a few hours, she was welded into her projectile until a workman with a short cutting arc would remove her after she had done her duty.

He picked up the entire projectile and slipped it into the ejection tube. He closed the door of the tube, spun the lock, seated himself in his chair, and put his own pin-set on.

Once again he flung the switch.

He sat in a small room, small, small, warm, warm, the bodies of the other three people moving close around him, the tangible lights in the ceiling bright and heavy against his closed eyelids.

As the pin-set warmed, the room fell away. The other people ceased to be people and became small glowing heaps of fire, embers, dark-red fire, with the consciousness of life burning like old red coals in a country fireplace.

As the pin-set warmed a little more, he felt Earth just below him, felt the ship slipping away, felt the turning Moon as it swung on the far side of the world, felt the planets and the hot, clear goodness of the Sun which kept the dragons so far from mankind's native ground.

Finally, he reached complete awareness.

He was telepathically alive to a range of millions of miles. He felt the dust which he had noticed earlier high above the ecliptic. With a thrill of warmth and tenderness, he felt the consciousness of the Lady May pouring over into his own. Her consciousness was as gentle and dear and yet sharp to the taste of his mind as if it were scented oil. It felt relaxing and reassuring. He could sense her welcome of him. It was scarcely a thought, just a raw emotion of greeting.

At last they were one again.

In a tiny remote corner of his mind, as tiny as the smallest toy he had ever seen in his childhood, he was still aware of the room and the ship, and of Father Moontree picking up a telephone and speaking to a Go-captain in charge of the ship.

His telepathic mind caught the idea long before his ears could frame the words. The actual sound followed the idea the way that thunder on an ocean beach follows the lightning inward from far out over the seas.

"The Fighting Room is ready. Clear to planoform, sir."

4. THE PLAY

Underhill was always a little exasperated the way that Lady May experienced things before he did.

He was braced for the quick vinegar thrill of planoforming, but he caught her report of it before his own nerves could register what happened.

Earth had fallen so far away that he groped for several milliseconds before he found the Sun in the upper rear right-hand corner of his telepathic mind.

That was a good jump, he thought. *This way well get there in four or five skips.*

A few hundred miles outside the ship, the Lady May thought back at him, *O warm, O generous, O gigantic man! O brave, O friendly, O tender and huge partner! O wonderful with you, with you so good, good, good, warm, warm, now to fight, now to go, good with you . . .*

He knew that she was not thinking words, that his mind took the dear amiable babble of her cat intellect and translated it into images which his own thinking could record and understand.

Neither one of them was absorbed in the game of mutual greetings. He reached out far beyond her range of perception to see if there was anything near the ship. It was funny how it was possible to do two things at once. He could scan space with his pin-set mind and yet at the same time catch a vagrant thought of hers, a lovely, affectionate thought about a son who had had a golden face and a chest covered with soft, incredibly downy white fur.

While he was still searching, he caught the warning from her. *We jump again!*

And so they had. The ship had moved to a second planoform. The stars were different. The sun was immeasurably far behind. Even the nearest stars were barely in contact. This was good dragon country, this open, nasty, hollow kind of space. He reached farther, faster, sensing and looking for danger, ready to fling the Lady May at danger wherever he found it.

Terror blazed up in his mind, so sharp, so clear, that it came through as a physical wrench.

The little girl named West had found something — something immense, long, black, sharp, greedy, horrific. She flung Captain Wow at it.

Underhill tried to keep his own mind clear. "Watch out!" he shouted telepathically at the others, trying to move the Lady May around.

At one corner of the battle, he felt the lustful rage of Captain Wow as the big Persian tomcat detonated lights while he approached the streak of dust which threatened the ship and the people within.

The lights scored near misses.

The dust flattened itself, changing from the shape of a sting ray into the shape of a spear.

Not three milliseconds had elapsed.

Father Moontree was talking human words and was saying in a voice that moved like cold molasses out of a heavy jar, "C-a-p-t-a-i-n." Underhill knew that the sentence was going to be "Captain, move fast!"

The battle would be fought and finished before Father Moontree got through talking.

Now, fractions of a millisecond later, the Lady May was directly in line.

Here was where the skill and speed of the partners came in. She could react faster than he. She could see the threat as an immense rat coming directly at her.

She could fire the lightbombs with a discrimination which he might miss.

He was connected with her mind, but he could not follow it.

His consciousness absorbed the tearing wound inflicted by the alien enemy. It was like no wound on Earth — raw, crazy pain which started like a burn at his navel. He began to writhe in his chair.

Actually he had not yet had time to move a muscle when the Lady May struck back at their enemy.

Five evenly spaced photonuclear bombs blazed out across a hundred-thousand miles.

The pain in his mind and body vanished.

He felt a moment of fierce, terrible, feral elation running through the mind of the Lady May as she finished her kill. It was always disappointing to the cats to find out that their enemies disappeared at the moment of destruction.

Then he felt her hurt, the pain and the fear that swept over both of them as the battle, quicker than the movement of an eyelid, had come and gone. In the same instant there came the sharp and acid twinge of planoform.

Once more the ship went skip.

He could hear Woodley thinking at him. "You don't have to bother much. This old son-of-a-gun and I will take over for a while."

Twice again the twinge, the skip.

He had no idea where he was until the lights of the Caledonia space-port shone below.

With a weariness that lay almost beyond the limits of thought, he threw his mind back into rapport with the pin-set, fixing the Lady May's projectile gently and neatly in its launching tube.

She was half dead with fatigue, but he could feel the beat of her heart, could listen to her panting, and he grasped the grateful edge of a *Thanks* reaching from her mind to his.

5. THE SCORE

They put him in the hospital at Caledonia.

The doctor was friendly but firm. "You actually got touched by that dragon. That's as close a shave as I've ever seen. It's all so quick that it'll be a long time before we know what happened scientifically, but I suppose you'd be ready for the insane asylum now if the contact had lasted several tenths of a millisecond longer. What kind of cat did you have out in front of you?"

Underhill felt the words coming out of him slowly. Words were such a lot of trouble compared with the speed and the joy of thinking, fast and sharp and clear, mind to mind! But words were all that could reach ordinary people like this doctor.

His mouth moved heavily as he articulated words. "Don't call our partners cats. The right thing to call them is partners. They fight for us in a team. You ought to know we call them partners, not cats. How is mine?"

"I don't know," said the doctor contritely. "We'll find out for you. Meanwhile, old man, you take it easy. There's nothing but rest that can help you. Can you make yourself sleep, or would you like us to give you some kind of sedative?"

"I can sleep," said Underhill. "I just want to know about the Lady May."

The nurse joined in. She was a little antagonistic. "Don't you want to know about the other people?"

"They're okay," said Underhill. "I knew that before I came in here."

He stretched his arms and sighed and grinned at them. He could see they were relaxing and were beginning to treat him as a person instead of a patient.

"I'm all right," he said. "Just let me know when I can go see my partner."

A new thought struck him. He looked wildly at the doctor. "They didn't send her off with the ship, did they?"

"I'll find out right away," said the doctor. He gave Underhill a reassuring squeeze of the shoulder and left the room.

The nurse took a napkin off a goblet of chilled fruit juice.

Underhill tried to smile at her. There seemed to be something wrong with the girl. He wished she would go away. First she had started to be friendly and now she was distant again. It's a nuisance being telepathic, he thought. You keep trying to reach even when you are not making contact.

Suddenly she swung around on him.

"You pinlighters! You and your damn cats!"

Just as she stamped out, he burst into her mind. He saw himself a radiant hero, clad in his smooth suede uniform, the pin-set crown shining like ancient royal jewels around his head. He saw his own face, handsome and masculine, shining out of her mind. He saw himself very far away and he saw himself as she hated him.

She hated him in the secrecy of her own mind. She hated him because he was — she thought — proud and strange and rich, better and more beautiful than people like her.

He cut off the sight of her mind and, as he buried his face in the pillow, he caught an image of the Lady May.

She is a cat, he thought. *That's all she is — a cat!*

But that was not how his mind saw her — quick beyond all dreams of speed, sharp, clever, unbelievably graceful, beautiful, wordless, and undemanding.

Where would he ever find a woman who could compare with her?

MARK ELF

I. Descent of a Lady

Stars wheeled silently over an early summer sky, even though men had long ago forgotten to call such nights by the name of June.

Laird tried to watch the stars with his eyes closed. It was a ticklish and terrifying game for a telepath: at any moment he might feel the heavens opening up and might, as his mind touched the image of the nearer stars, plunge himself into a nightmare of perpetual falling. Whenever he had this sickening, shocking, ghastly, suffocating feeling of limitless fall, he had to close his mind against telepathy long enough to let his powers heal.

He was reaching with his mind for objects just above the Earth, burnt-out space stations which flitted in their multiplex orbits, spinning forever, left over from the wreckage of ancient atomic wars.

He found one.

Found one so ancient it had no surviving cryotronic controls. Its design was archaic beyond belief; chemical tubes had apparently once lifted it out of Earth's atmosphere.

He opened his eyes and promptly lost it.

Closing his eyes he groped again with his seeking mind until he found the ancient derelict. As his mind reached for it again the muscles of his jaw tightened. He sensed life within it, life as old as the archaic machine itself.

In an instant, he made contact with his friend Tong Computer.

He poured his knowledge into Tong's mind. Keenly interested, Tong shot back at him an orbit which would cut the mildly parabolic pattern of the old device and bring it back down into Earth's atmosphere.

Laird made a supreme effort.

Calling on his unseen friends to aid him, he searched once more through the rubbish that raced and twinkled unseen just above the sky. Finding the ancient machine, he managed to give it a push.

In this fashion, about sixteen thousand years after she left Hit-

ler's Reich, Carlotta von Acht began her return to the Earth of men.

In all those years, she had not changed.
Earth had.

The ancient rocket tipped. Four hours later it had begun to graze the stratosphere, and its ancient controls, preserved by cold and time against all change, went back into effect. As they thawed, they became activated.

The course flattened out.

Fifteen hours later, the rocket was seeking a destination.

Electronic controls which had really been dead for thousands of years, out in the changeless time of space itself, began to look for German territory, seeking the territory by feedbacks which selected characteristic Nazi patterns of electronic communications scramblers.

There were none.

How could the machine know this? The machine had left the town of Pardubice, on April 2, 1945, just as the last German hideouts were being mopped up by the Red Army. How could the machine know that there was no Hitler, no Reich, no Europe, no America, no nations? The machine was keyed to German codes. Only German codes.

This did not affect the feedback mechanisms.

They looked for German codes anyway. There were none. The electronic computer in the rocket began to go mildly neurotic. It chattered to itself like an angry monkey, rested, chattered again, and then headed the rocket for something which seemed to be vaguely electrical. The rocket descended and the girl awoke.

She knew she was in the box in which her daddy had placed her. She knew that she was not a cowardly swine like the Nazis whom her father despised. She was a good Prussian girl of noble military family. She had been ordered to stay in the box by her father. What daddy told her to do she had always done. That was the first kind of rule for her kind of girl, a sixteen-year-old of the Junker class. The noise increased.

The electronic chattering flared up into a wild medley of

clicks.

She could smell something perfectly dreadful burning, something awful and rotten like flesh. She was afraid that it was herself, but she felt no pain.

"*Vadi, Vadi,* what is happening to me?" she cried to her father.

(Her father had been dead sixteen thousand and more years.
Obviously enough, he did not answer.)

The rocket began to spin. The ancient leather harness holding
her broke loose. Even though her section of the rocket was no bigger than a coffin, she was cruelly bruised.

She began to cry.

She vomited, even though very little came up. Then she slid in
her own vomit and felt nasty and ashamed because of something
which was a terribly simple human reaction.

The noises all met in a screaming, shrieking climax. The last
thing she remembered was the firing of the forward decelerators.
The metal had become fatigued so that the tubes not only fired
forward; they blew themselves to pieces sidewise as well.

She was unconscious when the rocket crashed. Perhaps that
saved her life, since the least muscular tension would have led to
the ripping of muscle and the crack of bone.

II. A Moron Found Her

His metals and plumes beamed in the moonlight as he scampered
about the dark forest in his gorgeous uniform. The government of
the world had long since been left to the Morons by the True Men,
who had no interest in such things as politics or administration.

Carlotta's weight, not her conscious will, had tripped the escape handle.

Her body lay half in, half out of the rocket.

She had gotten a bad burn on her left arm where her skin
touched the hot outer surface of the rocket.

The Moron parted the bushes and approached.

"I am the Lord High Administrator of Area Seventy-three," he
said, identifying himself according to the rules.

The unconscious girl did not answer. He rose up close to the rocket, crouching low lest the dangers of the night devour him, and listened intently to the radiation counter built in under the skin of his skull behind his left ear. He lifted the girl dextrously, flung her gently over his shoulder, turned about, ran back into the bushes, made a right-angle turn, ran a few paces, looked about him undecidedly, and then ran (still uncertain, still rabbit-like) down to the brook.

He reached into his pocket and found a burn-balm. He applied a thick coating to the burn on her arm. It would stay, killing the pain and protecting the skin, until the burn was healed.

He splashed cool water on her face. She awakened.

"*Wo bin ich?*" said she in German.

On the other side of the world, Laird, the telepath, had forgotten for the moment about the rocket. He might have understood her, but he was not there. The forest was around her and the forest was full of life, fear, hate, and pitiless destruction.

The Moron babbled in his own language.

She looked at him and thought that he was a Russian.

Said she in German, "Are you a Russian? Are you a German? Are you part of General Vlasov's army? How far are we from Prague? You must treat me courteously. I am an important girl . . ."

The Moron stared at her.

His face began to grin with innocent and consummate lust. (The True Men had never felt it necessary to inhibit the breeding habits of Morons. It was hard for any kind of human being to stay alive between the Beasts, the Unforgiven, and the Menschenjägers. The True Men wanted the Morons to go on breeding, to carry reports, to gather up a few necessaries, and to distract the other inhabitants of the world enough to let the True Men have the quiet and contemplation which their exalted but weary temperaments demanded.)

This Moron was typical of his kind. To him food meant eat, water meant drink, woman meant lust.

He did not discriminate.

Weary, confused, and bruised though she was, Carlotta still

recognized his expression.

Sixteen thousand years ago she had expected to be raped or murdered by the Russians. This soldier was a fantastic little man, plump and grinning, with enough medals for a Soviet colonel general. From what she could see in the moonlight, he was clean-shaven and pleasant, but he looked innocent and stupid to be so high-ranking an officer. Perhaps the Russians were all like that, she thought.

He reached for her.

Tired as she was, she slapped him.

The Moron was mixed up in his thoughts. He knew that he had the right to capture any Moron woman whom he might find. Yet he also knew that it was worse than death to touch any woman of the True Men. Which was this — this thing — this power — this entity who had descended from the stars?

Pity is as old and emotional as lust. As his lust receded, his elemental human pity took over. He reached in his jerkin pocket for a few scraps of food.

He held them out to her.

She ate, looking at him trustfully, very much the child.

Suddenly there was a crashing in the woods.

Carlotta wondered what had happened.

When she first saw him, his face had been full of concern. Then he had grinned and had talked. Later he had become lustful. Finally he had acted very much the gentleman. Now he looked blank, brain and bone and skin all concentrated into the act of listening — listening for something else, beyond the crashing, which she could not hear. He turned back to her.

"You must run. You must run. Get up and run. I tell you, run!"

She listened to his babble without comprehension.

Once again he crouched to listen.

He looked at her with blank horror on his face. Carlotta tried to understand what was the matter, but she could not riddle his meaning.

Three more strange little men dressed exactly like him came crashing out of the woods.

They ran like elk or deer before a forest fire. Their faces were blank with the exertion of running. Their eyes looked straight ahead so that they seemed almost blind. It was a wonder that they evaded the trees. They came crashing down the slope, scattering leaves as they ran. They splashed the waters of the brook as they stomped recklessly through it. With a half-animal cry Carlotta's Moron joined them.

The last she saw of him, he was running away into the woods, his plumes grinning ridiculously as his head nodded with the exertion of running.

From the direction from which the Morons had come, an unearthly creepy sound whistled through the woods. It was whistling, stealthy and low, accompanied by the very quiet sound of machinery.

The noise sounded like all the tanks in the world compressed into the living ghost of a tank, into the heart of a machine which survived its own destruction and, spiritlike, haunted the scenes of old battles.

As the sound approached Carlotta turned toward it. She tried to stand up and could not. She faced the danger. (All Prussian girls, destined to be the mothers of officers, were taught to face danger and never to turn their backs on it.) As the noise came close to her she could hear the high crazy inquiry of soft electronic chatter. It resembled the sonar she had once heard in her father's laboratory at the Reich's secret office's project Nordnacht.

The machine came out of the woods.

And it did look like a ghost.

III. The Death of All Men

Carlotta stared at the machine. It had legs like a grasshopper, a body like a ten-foot turtle, and three heads which moved restlessly in the moonlight.

From the forward edge of the top shell a hidden arm leapt forth, seeming to strike at her, deadlier than a cobra, quicker than a jaguar, more silent than a bat flitting across the face of the moon.

"Don't!" Carlotta screamed in German. The arm stopped suddenly in the moonlight.

The stop was so sudden that the metal twanged like the string of a bow.

The heads of the machine all turned toward her.

Something like surprise seemed to overtake the machine. The whistling dropped down to a soothing purr. The electronic chatter burst up to a crescendo and then stopped. The machine dropped to its knees.

Carlotta crawled over to it.

Said she in German, "What are you?"

"I am the death of all men who oppose the Sixth German Reich," said the machine in fluted singsong German. "If the Reichsangehöriger wishes to identify me, my model and number are written on my carapace."

The machine knelt at a height so low that Carlotta could seize one of the heads and look in the moonlight at the edge of the top shell. The head and neck, though made of metal, felt much more weak and brittle than she expected. There was about the machine an air of immense age.

"I can't see," wailed Carlotta. "I need a light."

There was the ache and grind of long-unused machinery. Another mechanical arm appeared, dropping flakes of near-crystallized dirt as it moved. The tip of the arm exuded light, blue, penetrating, and strange.

Brook, forest, small valley, machine, even herself, were all lit up by the soft penetrating blue light which did not hurt her eyes. The light even gave her a sense of well-being. With the light she could read. Traced on the carapace just above the three heads was this inscription:

WAFFENAMT DES SECHSTEN DEUTSCHEN REICHES
BURG EISENHOWER, A.D. 2495

And then below it in much larger Latin letters:

MENSCHENJÄGER MARK ELF

"What does 'Man-hunter, Model Eleven' mean?"

"That's me," whistled the machine. "How is it you don't know me if you are a German?"

"Of course, I'm a German, you fool!" said Carlotta. "Do I look like a Russian?"

"What is a Russian?" said the machine.

Carlotta stood in the blue light wondering, dreaming, dreading — dreading the unknown which had materialized around her.

When her father, Heinz Horst Ritter von Acht, professor and doctor of mathematical physics at project Nordnacht, had fired her into the sky before he himself awaited a gruesome death at the hands of the Soviet soldiery, he had told her nothing about the Sixth Reich, nothing about what she might meet, nothing about the future. It came to her mind that perhaps the world was dead, that the strange little men were not near Prague, that she was in Heaven or Hell, herself being dead, or if herself alive, was in some other world, or her own world in the future, or things beyond all human ken, or problems which no mind could solve . . .

She fainted again.

The Menschenjäger could not know that she was unconscious and addressed her in serious high-pitched singsong German. "German citizen, have confidence that I will protect you. I am built to identify German thoughts and to kill all men who do not have true German thoughts."

The machine hesitated. A loud chatter of electronic clicks echoed across the silent woods while the machine tried to compute its own mind. It was not easy to select from the long-unused store of words for so ancient and so new a situation. The machine stood in its own blue light. The only sound was the sound of the brook moving irresistibly about its gentle and unliving business. Even the birds in the trees and the insects round about were hushed into silence by the presence of the dreaded whistling machine.

To the sound-receptors of the Menschenjäger, the running of the Morons, by now some two miles distant, came as a very faint pitter-patter.

The machine was torn between two duties, the long-current and familiar duty of killing all men who were not German, and the ancient and forgotten duty of succoring all Germans, whoever they might be. After another period of electronic chatter, the machine began to speak again. Beneath the grind of its singsong German there was a curious warning, a reminder of the whistle which it made as it moved, a sound of immense mechanical and electronic effort.

Said the machine, "You are German. It has been long since there has been any German anywhere. I have gone around the world two thousand three hundred and twenty-eight times. I have killed seventeen thousand four hundred and sixty-nine enemies of the Sixth German Reich for sure, and I have probably killed forty-two thousand and seven additional ones. I have been back to the automatic restoration center eleven times. The enemies who call themselves the True Men always elude me. One of them I have not killed for more than three thousand years. The ordinary men whom some call the Unforgiven are the ones I kill most of all, but frequently I catch Morons and kill them, too. I am fighting for Germany, but I cannot find Germany anywhere. There are no Germans in Germany. There are no Germans anywhere. I accept orders from no one but a German. Yet there have been no Germans anywhere, no Germans anywhere, no Germans anywhere . . ."

The machine seemed to get a catch in its electronic brain because it went on repeating *no Germans anywhere* three or four hundred times.

Carlotta came to as the machine was dreamily talking to itself, repeating with sad and lunatic intensity, *no Germans anywhere.*

Said she, "I'm a German."

". . . no Germans anywhere, no Germans anywhere, except you, except you, except you."

The mechanical voice ended in a thin screech.

Carlotta tried to come to her feet.

At last the machine found words again. "What — do — I — do — now?"

"Help me," said Carlotta firmly.

This command seemed to tap an operable feedback in the ancient cybernetic assembly. "I cannot help you, member of the Sixth German Reich. For that you need a rescue machine. I am not a rescue machine. I am a hunter of men, designed to kill all the enemies of the German Reich."

"Get me a rescue machine then," said Carlotta.

The blue light went off, leaving Carlotta standing blinded in the dark. She was shaky on her legs. The voice of the Menschenjäger came to her.

"I am not a rescue machine. There are no rescue machines. There are no rescue machines anywhere. There is no Germany anywhere. There are no Germans anywhere, no Germans anywhere, no Germans anywhere, except you. You must ask a rescue machine. Now I go. I must kill men. Men who are enemies of the Sixth German Reich. That is all I can do. I can fight forever. I shall find a man and kill him. Then I shall find another man and kill him. I depart on the work of the Sixth German Reich."

The whistling and clicking resumed.

With incredible daintiness, the machine stepped as lightly as a cat across the brook. Carlotta listened intently in the darkness. Even the dry leaves of last year did not stir as the Menschenjäger moved through the shadow of the fresh leafy trees.

Abruptly there was silence.

Carlotta could hear the agonized clickety-clack of the computers in the Menschenjäger. The forest became a weird silhouette as the blue light went back on.

The machine returned.

Standing on the far side of the brook, it spoke to her in the dry, high-fluted singing German voice.

"Now that I have found a German I will report to you once every hundred years. That is correct. Perhaps that is correct. I do not know. I was built to report to officers. You are not an officer. Nevertheless you are a German. So I will report every hundred years. Meanwhile, watch out for the Kaskaskia Effect."

Carlotta, sitting again, was chewing some of the dry cubic food scraps which the Moron had left behind. They tasted like a mockery of chocolate. With her mouth full, she tried to shout to the Menschenjäger, "*Was ist das?*"

Apparently the machine understood, because it answered, "The Kaskaskia Effect is an American weapon. The Americans are all gone. There are no Americans anywhere, no Americans anywhere, no Americans anywhere — "

"Stop repeating yourself," said Carlotta. "What is that effect you are talking about?"

"The Kaskaskia Effect stops the Menschenjägers, stops the True Men, stops the Beasts. It can be sensed, but it cannot be seen or measured. It moves like a cloud. Only simple men with clean thoughts and happy lives can live inside it. Birds and ordinary beasts can live inside it, too. The Kaskaskia Effect moves about like clouds. There are more than twenty-one and less than thirty-four Kaskaskia Effects moving slowly about this planet Earth. I have carried other Menschenjägers back for restoration and rebuilding, but the restoration center can find no fault. The Kaskaskia Effect ruins us. Therefore, we run away . . . even though the officers told us to run from nothing. If we did not run away, we would cease to exist. You are a German. I think the Kaskaskia Effect would kill you. Now I go to hunt a man. When I find him I will kill him."

The blue light went off.

The machine whistled and clicked its way into the dark silence of the wooded night.

IV

Conversation with the Middle-Sized Bear

Carlotta was completely adult.

She had left the screaming uproar of Hitler Germany as it fell to ruins in its Bohemian outposts. She had obeyed her father, the Ritter von Acht, as he passed her and her sisters into missiles which had been designed as personnel and supply carriers for the First German National Socialist Moon Base.

He and his medical brother, Professor Doctor Joachim von Acht, had harnessed the girls securely in their missiles.

Their uncle the Doctor had given them shots.

Karla had gone first, then Juli, and then Carlotta.

Then the barbed-wire fortress of Pardubice and the monotonous grind of Wehrmacht trucks trying to escape the air strikes of the Red Air Force and the American fighter-bombers died in the one night, and this mysterious "forest in the middle of nothing-at-all" was born in the next night.

Carlotta was completely dazed.

She found a smooth-looking place at the edge of the brook. The old leaves were heaped high here. Without regard for further danger, she slept.

She had not been asleep more than a few minutes before the bushes parted again.

This time it was a bear. The bear stood at the edge of the darkness and looked into the moonlit valley with the brook running through it. He could hear no sound of Morons, no whistle of manshonyagger, as he and his kind called the hunting machines. When he was sure all was safe, he twitched his claws and reached delicately into a leather bag which was hanging from his neck by a thong. Gently he took out a pair of spectacles and fitted them slowly and carefully in front of his tired old eyes.

He then sat down next to the girl and waited for her to wake up.

She did not wake until dawn.

Sunlight and birdsong awakened her.

(Could it have been the probing of Laird's mind, whose far-reaching senses told him that a woman had magically and mysteriously emerged from the archaic rocket and that there was a human being unlike all the other kinds of mankind waking at a brookside in a place which had once been called Maryland?)

Carlotta awoke, but she was sick.

She had a fever.

Her back ached.

Her eyelids were almost stuck together with foam. The world had had time to develop all sorts of new allergenic substances since she had last walked on the surface of the Earth. Four civilizations had come and vanished. They and their weapons were sure to leave membrane-inflaming residue behind.

Her skin itched.

Her stomach felt upset.

Her arm was numb and covered with some kind of sticky black. She did not know it was a burn covered by the salve which the Moron had given her the previous night.

Her clothes were dry and seemed to be falling off her in

shreds.

She felt so bad that when she noticed the bear, she did not even have strength to run.

She just closed her eyes again.

Lying there with her eyes closed she wondered all over again where she was.

Said the bear in perfect German, "You are at the edge of the Unselfing Zone. You have been rescued by a Moron. You have stopped a Menschenjäger very mysteriously. For the first time in my own life I can see into a German mind and see that the word manshonyagger should really be Menschenjäger, a hunter of men. Allow me to introduce myself. I am the Middle-Sized Bear who lives in these woods."

The voice not only spoke German, but it spoke exactly the right kind of German. The voice sounded like the German which Carlotta had heard throughout her life from her father. It was a masculine voice, confident, serious, reassuring. With her eyes still closed she realized that it was a bear who was doing the talking. With a start, she recalled that the bear had been wearing spectacles.

Said she, sitting up, "What do *you* want?"

"Nothing," said the bear mildly.

They looked at each other for a while.

Then said Carlotta, "Who are you? Where did you learn German? What's going to happen to me?"

"Does the Fräulein," asked the bear, "wish me to answer the questions in order?"

"Don't be silly," said Carlotta. "I don't care what order. Anyhow, I'm hungry. Do you have anything I could eat?"

The bear responded gently, "You wouldn't like hunting for insect grubs. I have learned German by reading your mind. Bears like me are friends of the True Men and we are good telepaths. The Morons are afraid of us, but we are afraid of the manshonyaggers. Anyhow, you don't have to worry very much because your husband is coming soon."

Carlotta had been walking down toward the brook to get a drink. His last words stopped her in her tracks.

"My husband?" she gasped.

"So probably that it is certain. There is a True Man named Laird who has brought you down. He already knows what you are thinking, and I can see his pleasure in finding a human being who is wild and strange, but not really wild and not really strange. At this moment he is thinking that you may have left the centuries to bring the gift of vitality back among mankind. He is thinking that you and he will have wonderful children. Now he is telling me not to tell you what I think he thinks, for fear that you will run away." The bear chuckled.

Carlotta stood, her mouth agape.

"You may sit in my chair," said the Middle-Sized Bear, "or you can wait here until Laird comes to get you. Either way you will be taken care of. Your sickness will heal. Your ailments will go away. You will be happy again. I know this because I am one of the wisest of all known bears."

Carlotta was angry, confused, frightened, and sick again. She started to run.

Something as solid as a blow hit her.

She knew without being told that it was the bear's mind reaching out and encompassing hers.

It hit — boom! — and that was all.

She had never before stopped to think of how comfortable a bear's mind was. It was like lying in a great big bed and having mother take care of one when one was a very little girl, glad to be petted and sure of getting well.

The anger poured out of her. The fear left her. The sickness began to lighten. The morning seemed beautiful.

She herself felt beautiful as she turned —

Out of the blue sky, dropping swiftly but gracefully, came the figure of a bronze young man. A happy thought pulsed against her mind. *That is Laird, my beloved. He is coming. He is coming. I shall be happy forever after.*

It *was* Laird.

And so she was.

ABOUT THE AUTHOR

Cordwainer Smith was the pseudonym used by Paul Myron Anthony Linebarger (1913-1966) for his science fiction works. Linebarger was a noted East Asia scholar and expert in psychological warfare.

Linebarger also employed the literary pseudonyms "Carmichael Smith" (for his political thriller *Atomsk*), "Anthony Bearden" (for his poetry) and "Felix C. Forrest" (for the novels *Ria* and *Carola*).

"Scanners Live in Vain" was Linebarger's first published SF story as an adult (his short story "War No. 81-Q," which he wrote at age 15 was published in his high school magazine), and the first appearance of the Cordwainer Smith pen name. It was written in 1945, and had been rejected by a number of magazines before its acceptance and publication in *Fantasy Book* in 1950. It was in that obscure magazine that it was noticed by SF writer Frederik Pohl who, impressed with the story's powerful imagery and style, subsequently re-published it in 1952 in the more widely read anthology *Beyond the End of Time*.

www.ingramcontent.com/pod-product-compliance
Lightning Source LLC
Chambersburg PA
CBHW020143150626
46552CB00021B/1395